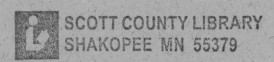

A Place to Belong

A Place to Belong

by Emily Crofford

Carolrhoda Books, Inc./Minneapolis

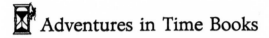 Adventures in Time Books

LIBRARY OF CONGRESS CATALOGING-IN-PUBLICATION DATA

Crofford, Emily.
  A place to belong / by Emily Crofford.
    p. cm.
  Summary: In 1935, after his family loses their farm and is forced to move onto
an Arkansas plantation, sixth grader Talmadge struggles to endure their harsh
new life and fights to stay in school against his mother's wishes.
  ISBN 0-87614-808-9
  [1. Depressions—1929—Fiction. 2. Arkansas—Fiction.] I. Title.
PZ7.C873p1   1993
[Fic]—dc20   93-9289
                                                                CIP
                                                                 AC

Manufactured in the United States of America

1 2 3 4 5 6 – P/BP – 99 98 97 96 95 94

In memory of L.H. Autry

Chapter 1

Talmadge turned over again. Across the room, Dwight had been sleep-breathing for what seemed like an hour. Mama and Papa, who slept in the front room next to his and Dwight's bedroom, hadn't turned in yet. They were in the kitchen; now and then he heard the murmur of their voices.

Lights flashed on the wall; a vehicle had turned into the yard. The lights went off. Talmadge quickly crawled to the foot of his bed and peered through the window. There was not much moon, but he could tell that it was a car, not a truck. It was Cousin Maybelle and her husband Mr. Parks's A-Model Ford! They had driven all the way from Sweet Spring at night? They weren't coming to the front door; they were walking around to the kitchen door.

Shivering from the cold, Talmadge got back under the covers. He heard a stir of greetings, then there was only Mr. Parks's voice. He couldn't make out the words, but whatever they were, they had caused Papa to moan. Mr. Parks and Cousin Maybelle had a telephone! Maybe Grandpa or Grandma McLinn, who lived a good hundred miles east of Sweet Spring, was bad sick.

No, that wasn't it; Mama was keeping her voice in check, but she was furious about something. The old feud between Mama's and Papa's families had probably broken out again. Cousin Maybelle was the only McLinn who befriended Mama, and none of Mama's family, the Thorntons, befriended Papa.

Mr. Parks and Cousin Maybelle were leaving, going out through the front door. Papa was coming toward his and Dwight's room. The door opened.

"Put on your clothes, and your shoes and socks," Papa said. "Then go back to the kitchen where it's warm." He went to Dwight's bed. "Get up, son," he said. "We got trouble."

It wasn't the feud; it was something serious. A pang of jealousy went through Talmadge. He was the one who had been lying here worrying, but it was to Dwight that Papa said, "We got trouble."

Except for Missy, who was only four and still asleep, they all sat at the kitchen table. The clock, which sat on a shelf near the cookstove, showed ten after nine. Talmadge fidgeted while Papa organized his thoughts.

Roseanne, who was sixteen, two years older than Dwight, hadn't combed her hair, and she looked sleepy. But even with her eyelids drooping and her hair tousled, she was pretty. Mama, who was five feet, eight inches tall, big-boned, and a little plump but not fat, was clearly still simmering.

"Between hard times and a poor market for chewing tobacco," Papa finally said, "I ain't been able to keep up the payments on our place." He looked down at the backs of his bony hands, which lay on the table. "The sheriff will be coming tomorrow to notify me that we've been foreclosed on."

The clock's ticking banged against the walls. Then, in a harsh, bitter voice, Dwight said, "I thought President Roosevelt was going to do away with hard times."

"Well, he was just inaugurated ten months ago," Talmadge said. "He ain't hardly had time to get everything straightened out."

Papa shook his head as a way of telling them this was not the time to argue politics. "We got work to do tonight," he said. "If the livestock and equipment ain't sold by the time the sheriff and Old Man Mosely get here tomorrow, they won't just take back the house and land Mosely sold us. They can take all our equipment. And our stock."

"They can't take our household furnishings," Mama said. "That's against the law. And Mr. Parks bought the hauling truck whilst him and Maybelle was here tonight. He give Papa twenty dollars for it and they signed a paper to show Mr. Parks owns it now. If he chooses to let your daddy use it, there's not a thing the law can do about it." She glanced at Papa, who kept looking down at the table, then went on. "We'll sell our mules for a dollar each tonight. Sell the plows for a nickel apiece, and so on. There's some rent acreages and vacant houses around. Soon's we get settled, we'll buy everything back at the same price. It's been done before. So you see, it ain't the end of the world."

Talmadge cringed. Papa had bought this place before he was born, and it had always made him proud. Everybody would know what had happened; he dreaded going to school tomorrow.

Papa raised his head and said to Mama, "Pet, I'd as soon sell what we can for real. Be shed of Wild Hog Holler, and for that matter, Rim County. And I'd like for us to be gone before the sheriff comes to read the paper and put up the sign."

Mama swallowed as if she had a mighty lump in her throat. Then she put her hand on top of Papa's and nodded.

Talmadge thought it was just as well that Ben, their

collie, had died right after Christmas. Ben would never have been able to adjust to a different place.

Papa scraped back his chair, stood, and began to pace. "Dwight, take Babe and Joe over to the Captain. He's always envied me that team of mules, and he don't trust banks, so he'll have cash. He'll pay us as much as he can afford. Tell him our cow and calf, the hogs, chickens, and all our equipment are for sale," Papa went on. "Tonight. Ask him who he knows south of here in Tennessee—or Alabama or Mississippi, for that matter—could use some good workers. On the way home, stop and tell a few other folks we're having a sale. Talmadge, go the other direction and tell the Listons."

"He ought not be walking that rough road at night," Mama said. "I'll go tell the Listons."

"I'll take a lantern, Mama," Talmadge said. "I'll be careful." He knew she had his best interest at heart, but she babied him too much because of his clubfoot.

"Papa," Roseanne said in a low voice, "you told Dwight to take Joe and Babe, but you never mentioned Ella."

Papa shook his head. In a tired, sad voice, he said, "Ella is too old and feeble to be made to do anything but light work. I don't know anybody I'd trust her to."

Roseanne began to cry.

"We don't have time for that," Mama said sharply as she rose from the table.

Talmadge put on his coat and cap and went out the front door. He was a quarter of a mile up the road when he heard the shot, and one shrill, dying bray. He shivered, but not from the cold. He wouldn't think about Old Ella. He would think about how, like Papa, he wanted to be gone from here. And he never wanted to come back.

Chapter 2

Talmadge's mind floated to the awakening edge of sleep. He snuggled farther down under the quilts, and went back into light, dreaming sleep. Dwight was speaking to him in the dream, saying words Talmadge couldn't make out, and there was something akin to hate in his voice.

He didn't like this dream; he wanted to wake up. He forced his eyes to open. For a moment, he was disoriented, then it all came back. They had left the place in Mississippi the Captain had sent them to a year ago when they lost their farm. They were moving again,

and he and Dwight were lying on stacked mattresses
with their heads at the cab end of the truck bed. Light
filtered through the quilt over his head.

They were going to Limon Plantation in northeast
Arkansas. The plantation's hub had used to be a log-
ging town, a hobo had told Papa. Great trees had grown
in the whole area, he said, but now the trees were gone
and the rich land had been turned to growing crops.
"And they're still clearing," he said, "making new
ground." The hobo had told Papa that Limon was much
larger than the place in Mississippi. "Two hundred
families live there," he had said, "and it covers three
thousand acres. If I were a farming man with a family,
that's where I would go."

Papa had written a letter to Mr. Limon, who wrote
back that there was work and a vacant house for the
McLinns.

The sound and feel beneath the tires changed; Papa
had turned off the highway onto a gravel road. They
must be there. If he sat up, he could see over the top
truck slat. But if he disturbed Dwight, he'd likely get
clobbered. He was going to take the chance. Carefully, he pushed the quilts down, sat up, and gasped when
the late-afternoon January air stung his face and pene-
trated his shirt and long johns.

The houses on both sides of the road, which was
bound to be the main road, ranged from big, comfortable-looking places down to box and shotgun houses.

A box house was four rooms arranged in the shape of a box. A shotgun house was called that because the rooms were in a row; you could shoot through the front door and the bullet would go through every door in the house.

All of the houses had front, back, and side yards, which was a good sign. Mr. Limon wasn't so hungry for profit that he put every available foot of land into crops.

Dwight turned over, and Jasper, the stray dog that had taken up with Talmadge in Mississippi, roused himself to crawl from beneath a kitchen chair near the back end of the truck. Talmadge shook his head; Jasper lay back down and gazed up at him with his wet Spaniel eyes.

There weren't any folks to see. Everybody was inside, out of the cold. No, there was a man chopping wood in his backyard. Two houses farther on, a colored boy going to the pump with a bucket turned around and stared.

Papa was stopping. "Howdy," Talmadge heard him say.

"Evening," a man's quiet voice replied.

Talmadge wished he could see the man, who would be standing by the cab on the driver's side, but to do so, he would have to crawl to the side of the mattress, get on his knees, and bend out over the top slat. That would for sure wake Dwight.

Now Papa was introducing himself and asking directions.

The man said his name was Matt Williams. "Mr. Limon told us y'all were coming," he said. "Just keep following this road till it ends."

"Is the school on this road?" Roseanne asked in her shy, sweet voice.

"School? Why, no, Miss, it's—the school is...."

Talmadge grinned. Mr. Williams was puzzled to the point of stumbling because a woman of seventeen had asked about the school. He didn't know Talmadge was in the back and that Roseanne was asking for his sake.

Mr. Williams cleared his throat. "If you take a left at the next crossroad, you'll make a loop past the school and come back out further down on this same road."

"Much obliged," Papa said, and pulled off.

A thin veil of dust rose behind the truck, but it was easy enough to see that the man was years younger than Papa. Two children, a girl about four and a boy probably going on three, were with him.

They wouldn't go by the school. Mama and Papa would be anxious to get to the house. He settled back down under the quilts, but he could tell when the gravel thinned beneath the tires. Now they were on a dirt road. It was getting rougher, and the truck bounced in the ruts. Papa was making a strong left across a shallow ditch. The truck stopped; Papa turned off the motor.

Talmadge pushed back his side of the quilts. "I reckon we're arrived."

Dwight sat up, shivered, and ran his fingers through his thick brown hair. "That's lucky for you," he said. "Another half mile of you fidgeting and I'd of clobbered you." He swung off the mattresses, and went over the side of the truck.

Talmadge retied his shoelaces, crawled to the foot of the mattresses, and slowly slid down them. When his feet met the truck bed, his sleeping right foot, his clubfoot, tingled, then hurt so bad he bit his lip. He picked Jasper up, and with his left arm wrapped around the dog, worked his way through furniture, and climbed over the side of the truck. Clinging to the top slat with his right hand, he looked down, then let go. He landed on his feet, but crumpled to his knees.

He turned Jasper loose, grasped the back tire, and pulled himself up. There were all kinds of clubfeet, some worse than his. Barefoot, his heel wouldn't touch the ground, and his weight fell on the little toe and its neighbor. But he could walk okay, even run a little when he was wearing his shoes, thanks to the built-up heel Papa put on the right one.

He looked around for Jasper, saw him going into the scraggly, cutover woods that came up to the yard. His family stood gazing at the house. Papa's rounded shoulders slumped even more than usual because he had been driving for five hours. Mama stood as straight as ever. Some of her fine, brown hair had come out of the soft roll she made around her head, and the wind tossed the loose strands.

Dwight stood by Roseanne, his wide right shoulder touching her narrow left shoulder. Missy stood on the outside, next to Mama. Her yellow hair was tangled and she looked as worn out as the rag doll she held in her left hand. When Talmadge walked up beside her, she put her right arm around his thighs and leaned her head into his side.

They all gazed silently at the never-painted house. The second of the steps leading to a buckling porch lay on the ground.

"Won't take much to fix the steps," Papa said. "Or the porch either." He considered for a moment. "I could do a lot with this house. It's cypress. Hard, durable wood."

Papa was good at carpentry. Back in Wild Hog Holler he had not only kept their house in good repair, he had practically rebuilt the barn.

"It's a day worker house, Warren," Mama said. "You don't have the liberty to put a nail in it."

After a silence, Papa said, "You remember, Mr. Limon wrote that there were a cookstove and heater in it."

"It's a house," Dwight said. "And Papa and me have got work."

Talmadge winced. Dwight had not gone back to school after they left Wild Hog Holler. This was not the first time he had pointed out that he worked, leaving unspoken but clear his anger that Talmadge not only continued to go to school, but seldom missed a day. Mama also thought he should consider quitting. She knew how hard it had been for him at the school in Mississippi; she was probably figuring he wouldn't go here. It would behoove him to make his stand right now. "Papa, ought I start school tomorrow?"

Papa mulled it over. Papa always mulled over a question before he answered. "Today's Wednesday, ain't it?"

"Yes," Roseanne said. "It's Wednesday, January 10. The Year of Our Lord, 1935." With a lilt in her voice, she added, "A new beginning. I think we're going to like it here. The main road has a contented feel about it."

Talmadge was about to say he agreed, when Papa said, "Why don't you wait till Monday to start to school. That'll give us time to settle in and get the lay of the place."

"Yes, sir."

Turning on his heel, Dwight said, "We don't have much daylight left." He climbed into the truck, found the bucket, and handed it down to Mama. Inside the bucket were a can of lye and a jar of priming water. Even if the house had been left spotless, Mama would scrub it down before she let Papa and Dwight bring in the furnishings. He gave the broom and cleaning rags to Roseanne. He dropped the ax, a razor-sharp double blade, to the ground in front of Talmadge.

He couldn't keep from flinching, but he didn't look up at Dwight, who would likely have a mocking glitter in his eyes.

Mama and Roseanne and Missy were going into the house; Talmadge went around it. Good. The last people to live here had left a small stack of cookstove wood on the porch. His eyes moved over the sizable backyard to a one-hole toilet and a small chicken house, the only outbuildings.

Mama came out the door. Her face reacted to the lack of a barn, then she looked beyond the yard. "It's mean-looking country."

Talmadge gazed at what had been forestland. Winter-dry vines climbed over huge stumps. Tall browned grasses bent with the wind, and trees the loggers had passed over, willows and sweet gums, grew alongside spindly oak and hickory saplings.

Mama came down the steps and gazed eastward.

"You still homesick, Mama?"

"I miss the beauty, yes. The cedar and dogwood. The streams. I miss visiting with other women, quilting together and all. And having a cow and chickens." After a moment, she said in a low voice, "And even with the hard feelings between your daddy's family and mine, I miss Tennessee." She shook herself and looked at him. "You aim to go to school here, then?"

"Yessum. I do." He hoped the sixth grade here was not ahead of the one in Mississippi.

Mama went back up the steps and began picking up wood. "I'll start a fire in the kitchen stove. When you've chopped an armload of wood for the heater, leave the ax and bring it on in. The wind's whiffling through the walls in yonder."

"Yessum," Talmadge said, and left. They surely

wouldn't stay out here long. The plantation owner would see what good workers Papa and Dwight were and let them move into a better house.

Chapter 3

Saws sang, axes thudded, and kaiser blades swished in the cutover woods and thickets as Talmadge left to go to school. He knew the way; Friday he and Papa had gone to the store and to the school. Papa had talked to Mr. Whitis, the superintendent. Mr. Whitis had only asked a few questions, then enrolled Talmadge.

A stump-blowing dynamite blast tore the air. Talmadge shuddered and murmured a prayer for Papa and Dwight and the other men. The uncleared land fell behind him. Stalk cutters had rolled here; mangled corn stalks stuck out of the ground at odd angles. Papa said corn was always planted first in new ground because it was a grass.

He reached land where cotton had grown last year. A bone-skinny boy about his age came out of the house just ahead of him. Looking straight ahead, the boy angled across his yard, and walked fast up the road.

The boy turned onto the road that went past the post office and the Limon Store. By the time Talmadge made the turn, the boy was well ahead of him. He reached the edge of a bayou. The bayou, he had learned on Saturday, was caused by the New Madrid Earthquake of 1811, and it was fed by a natural spring.

The boy turned left onto the road that went past the school. Despite the cold, Talmadge's palms began to sweat. He passed the Limon family's comfortable-looking homes. The day the McLinns arrived, he had seen some nice houses on the main road, but they weren't painted white like these houses. The important lumber people must have lived here; huge trees graced the yards and filled a small park.

He made the left and saw the school, a long one-story brick building with a gracious plenty of ground space. The only other building was a two-story stucco on the other side of the school. It used to be the school, Mr. Whitis had said, but he and his family now lived there.

At the point where the sidewalk met the road, he stopped walking. There weren't many little kids in the west side yard with swings and seesaws. They must be inside, out of the cold. Quite a few older students were in the front yard. Some of them stared at him. He could understand why; the too-long overcoat a teacher had given him last winter made him look like a scarecrow. He took a deep breath and stepped onto the sidewalk.

He had hoped that his teacher, Miss Gibson, wouldn't make him stand in front of the class, but she did. "We have a new pupil," she said. "This is Talmadge McLinn from the mountains of east Tennessee."

Rim County wasn't in east Tennessee, it was in middle Tennessee, but he couldn't correct a teacher. "From Wild Hog Holler to be exact," he said. The story went that the name had come about because a long time back a man had been calling in his hogs and his friend had said, "That's not just a hog holler—that's a *wild hog holler.*"

In an audible whisper, a boy asked, "Did he say Wild Hog Holler?!" There were snickers and smothered laughter. Some students pretended to be looking down at their notebooks, but they were really looking at his foot. A boy in a front desk gazed into his face and smirked.

Sweat ran down from his armpits. He must look as funny as he sounded. His hair was too long, not clipped short up the back of his neck like the other boys' hair. And none of them were wearing overalls. They were wearing either khaki or corduroy britches. Miss Gibson tapped her ruler. "Class! I'm ashamed of you!" She assigned him a desk, and he stumbled to it.

When morning recess came, some of the girls smiled at him as they left the room. A cross-eyed girl stepped over and spoke to him. "I'm LaVerne." In a low voice, she said, "Watch out for Ambrose—better known as Stinky. He's mean as a snake." She left and caught up with some other girls. The boy he had seen this morning who lived on the same road he did, and a tall, fine-looking boy wearing corduroy britches and a white shirt, came up to him. "I'm John Edward," the tall boy said. "And this is Peadod."

"I'm glad to meet y'all." He had learned in Mississippi to say "y'all" instead of "you'ens" when addressing more than one person. "I saw you this morning when you came out of your house," he said to Peadod. "I don't live too far yonder side of you."

Peadod, who had big ears and a thin face, as well as the skinny body, looked at the door. "Yeah," he said. "Y'all just moved in." He shifted his weight from one foot to the other. "I was in a hurry this morning."

At least, Talmadge thought, Peadod hadn't pretended that he didn't see him coming.

"I got to go to the bathroom," Peadod said, and quickly walked away.

John Edward stayed with him while they got their coats from the rack in the hall. But when they went outside, other students, boys and girls, asked John

Edward to join them in a game of "Wolf Over the River." Watching them go, Talmadge took his cap from his coat pocket and put it on.

He started walking down the sidewalk so he would have a closer view of the game. Stinky was coming toward him. Talmadge stiffened.

"I sure like your cap," Stinky said. "How about letting me try it on?"

He faked a smile and shook his head. "I don't think it'll fit you."

"I bet it will," Stinky said. He grabbed the cap, and as Talmadge reached for it, tossed it to another boy, who in turn threw it to a different boy. Looking inside the cap, the boy's eyes widened as if in horror—as if there were lice in the cap. He threw it to the ground. Stinky laughed and slapped the boy on the back.

Miss Gibson was charging toward them. Talmadge quickly picked up his cap. "It's all right, Miss Gibson," he said. "They was just funnin'." But she yelled at the boys, and most of her fury was directed toward Stinky. When she left, Stinky, whose face had turned red, glared at Talmadge, then spat on the ground and walked away.

He knew Miss Gibson hadn't meant to make things harder for him. But she had. He would have to stay out of Stinky's way for a while.

Talmadge leaned back against the sun-warmed wall on the side of the building where the children played. None of the other sixth-graders, except John Edward sometimes, came here. For two weeks he had avoided trouble by mostly staying inside during recess and lunch periods. Sometimes he worked on his lessons, or read the book that Cousin Maybelle and Mr. Parks had given to him. Once he talked with a girl in his class, Meg Weston, who had an earache and had to stay inside.

He took his harmonica from his overall bib pocket and played quietly while he considered his situation. He never wanted to fight, for two reasons. The first was the hurt caused by the old feud between Mama's and Papa's families. Papa said it went all the way back to the fourteenth century wars in Scotland when the McLinns and Thorntons fought on opposite sides. The other reason was that he changed inside himself when he got mad. In general, the class now accepted his presence. If he were careful not to give Stinky or any of Stinky's buddies an excuse to get mad at him, maybe he could make it.

The bell rang and he went inside. He passed Miss Gibson and another teacher, talking in the hall. As he entered the classroom, Stinky stepped in front of him. He couldn't stop quickly enough. He bumped into Stinky.

Stinky whirled around. "Why don't you watch where

you're going?" He continued to glare at Talmadge after he reached his desk. "Did you see that?" he asked C.C., the boy across the aisle from him, in a voice loud enough to carry around the room. "Hillbilly pushed me."

Miss Gibson appeared in the doorway; silence fell, then there was a stir as the class got out their health books. "I didn't catch what you said as I came in, Ambrose," Miss Gibson said.

Some of the girls snickered, as they always did when Miss Gibson addressed Stinky. Having a name like Ambrose, Talmadge thought, probably had something to do with Stinky's becoming a bully.

With an injured tone implying that she had misjudged him, Stinky motioned toward his opened health book. "I was just saying this was an interesting chapter."

It wouldn't do any good to apologize to Stinky. He had done that at the school in Mississippi. The class had decided he was weak and made his life even more miserable. His hand trembled as he picked up his pencil to make notes.

When the last bell rang and he went outside, Stinky and his buddies stood halfway between the building and the road. Talmadge stepped off the sidewalk; he would cut across the grounds, hit the road up near the corner.

It wasn't going to work; they were coming. Silently, he gave himself a command: Don't look back, and don't walk faster. If he showed fear, they might gang up on him.

"Hey, Hillbilly," Stinky called, "why're you in such a hurry to get out to the Newground?"

Stinky was not the only one who said it as if it were a place apart from Limon. It wasn't new ground yet anyway.

A chill went down his spine. They were right behind him. Stinky stepped in front of him. "This must be a real good book," he said, and took hold of Talmadge's book, his *Bob, Son of Battle.* "How about letting me borrow it?"

Stinky shouldn't have touched his book; the anger was there now, pressing inside his chest. "I don't lend it," he said, and heard the harshness in his voice.

Stinky blinked, then yanked the book out of his hand. "Sure you do."

"Give it back!"

Stinky looked baffled now, unsure of himself, and for a second Talmadge thought he might not have to fight Stinky. Yes, he would. Stinky couldn't back down in front of his buddies. Others were also here now. More were coming.

Chapter 4

Stinky threw the book on the ground. "You want it, Hillbilly, you...."

Talmadge didn't wait for the rest; he shucked his coat, forced himself to wait until Stinky had shed his own coat. The second Stinky was ready, Talmadge swung with his right. A teacher at the last school had taught him about a spot high on the jaw that could put down even a powerful opponent.

When Stinky reeled, the crowd gasped; a murmur swelled to commotion, and a boy's low voice said, "Get him, Talmadge!" But those things seemed far away. He had to concentrate on keeping himself in control, had to hold at bay his blood lust because Stinky was off balance.

Stinky circled, stepped in, and made a quick jab. Talmadge didn't feel the pain; he only knew Stinky's fist had hit his nose because blood ran warm over his mouth. He couldn't circle as Stinky was doing; his bad foot would trip him up. He waited.

Stinky stepped in closer; he intended to jab again. Talmadge swung. Stinky went down. Some of the girls screamed, and he heard the voice again, low and close: "Now!"

He straddled Stinky, raised his fist, and stared into frightened eyes. His senses came back, the fury drained out of him, and as he clumsily got to his feet, he began to cry.

The crowd was quiet, as if in shock, while he put on his coat, but after he walked away, a boy yelled, "Go back to Wild Hog Holler!" Others took up the call. Talmadge took the handkerchief from his overcoat pocket and wiped away the blood. His nose was sore, but that was nothing compared to the hurt in his chest. It was an awful thing to be despised.

He had reached the bayou when a memory came into his mind. Jasper was half-starved, bleeding, fighting for his life against a pack of other stray dogs. Talmadge had picked up a sturdy stick and struck some hard blows before the dogs came to their senses and scattered. The students who had yelled "Go back to Wild Hog Holler" didn't despise him. He was an outsider; he had been crying and bleeding, and he hadn't made Stinky admit defeat.

By the time he reached home, he thought he might fall down from weariness. And his feet ached from the cold. He turned into his yard, past Mama's green jars that she had set along the path to keep out bad spirits, and past the truck. It hadn't been out of the yard since they arrived here. Limon didn't have a filling station. Dwight said there was one up the highway, but Papa said there was enough gas left in the tank in case of an emergency, and otherwise, they could walk anywhere they needed to go.

Jasper didn't run to greet him. Mama, who said dogs were meant to stay outside, must have weakened again and let Jasper come inside. He wished he could keep Mama from knowing he had been in a fight. Maybe he could keep the coat on until he got back to his room. He could change his shirt and, when he had a chance, wash out the blood.

As he pulled the front door closed behind him, Missy and Jasper came running. Missy threw her arms around his waist, and Talmadge leaned down and kissed the top of her head. Her hair smelled of soap and shone like corn silks. Missy had been born before her time and Mama had been sick for weeks afterward. When you had fed and rocked a baby, the baby became your child, too, so all of them had a special feeling for her.

He patted Jasper, laid his book on the sewing machine, and let out a sigh. The heater glowed red at the sides; the fragrance of burning oak mingled with the mouth-watering smell of simmering great northern beans. "Sure is good to be home," he said as he headed for his room to the left of the kitchen. Before he was halfway across the front room, Mama came from the kitchen. She probed his face with a straight, unblinking gaze. She couldn't know. He had wiped away all the blood or Missy would have said something.

"Take off your coat and stay a while," Mama said.

He hesitated, then removed the coat. Missy gasped.

"Ain't nothing to worry about. Just a nosebleed." It wasn't actually a lie. "Where's Roseanne?"

"She went to stay with Mr. Williams's children," Missy said.

"The Mr. Williams who gave us directions the day we arrived?"

Missy nodded. "The regular lady couldn't make it to keep them today while Mr. Williams was working. Roseanne said poor Mrs. Williams died of spidal something."

"Spinal meningitis," Mama said.

He didn't have to look; he could feel her eyes still boring into him. He raised his eyes to meet hers. "Fight," he said.

Mama's mouth made a tight line. "Come on in the kitchen."

When he had pulled a chair out from the table and sat down, she touched his nose at various places. "Ain't broke. Take off that there shirt so I can soak out the blood. Missy, you'll find his handkerchief in his right coat pocket. Bring it in here."

Talmadge unbuckled his overall straps and removed his shirt. Holding it with her thumb and forefinger, Missy brought the bloody handkerchief.

"For the life of me," Mama said, "I can't fathom why you keep letting yourself in for this. You've already got half a year higher in school than your daddy or your brother did."

He didn't answer. Mama didn't understand his need to learn.

"Get a couple of cookies and take a rest afore you do your chores," Mama said.

As he went into his room, she banged the soaking pan down on the table and said to the Lord, "I'd be obliged you'd see fit to get us off this forsaken place!"

Talmadge closed his door. "I'd be obliged you don't." He would have to go through the same thing at another place, which might not be as promising as Limon. And he kept hearing the muted voice in his mind's ear. Somebody had wanted him to whip Stinky.

He put his harmonica on the chest of drawers he and Dwight shared, sat down on his bed, took off his shoes and socks, and massaged his bad foot. When he had removed his overalls, he lay down, pulled the quilt over himself, put his hands beneath his head, and gazed at the ceiling. Peadod! It had been Peadod's voice. He had probably been Stinky's goat at some point. Peadod had been nervous about staying behind with John Edward to greet him the day he started school here, and still didn't walk with him. He had spoken in a low voice today so others couldn't hear him above the hubbub.

Talmadge turned on his side. He would know tomorrow morning what kind of person Peadod was. If Peadod waited for him, they would become friends. If he didn't wait, he wasn't worth thinking about.

Chapter 5

They were into March, but mornings were still chilly. Talmadge hunkered down under the covers. He had to get up; Peadod would be waiting for him. He had a buddy.

The daydream floated beneath his closed eyelids: he was smiling benignly as boys crowded around him.

He opened his eyes, threw off the covers, and got up. Across the room, Dwight's bed was neatly made. Dwight and Papa had left for work two hours ago. He made his bed, but it didn't look very neat. He shrugged. Even when he tried hard he couldn't make a bed as well as Dwight could, and this morning he didn't have time to try. Besides, he was shivering. He put on his shirt and reached for his overalls.

When he went into the warm kitchen, Mama was not there. He heard Roseanne stirring in her room, heard Missy sigh with the pulling up from sleep. He stepped onto the back porch. Mama stood in the yard, gazing at the sky, which had a strange, dirty-red cast. The few Plymouth Rock chickens that Peadod's mother had given to them looked unsettled.

"You ain't going to school today," Mama said to him.

"I've got to go to school. If I don't...." He stopped. He couldn't say that if he didn't, tomorrow or the day after she would find another reason to keep him home. He went to the toilet, came back to the pump, and washed his hands and face in the icy water. "Maybe somebody's burning off brush somewhere," he said as he came up the porch steps.

"And maybe the good Lord's decided to get rid of this here wicked world."

"Mama, about school...."

"You ain't going!"

Roseanne and Missy were in the kitchen when he and Mama went inside. Missy, still sleep-drugged, ate a bowl of oatmeal. Roseanne paced. Mama ripped strings out of a flour sack to make a dish towel. "Sure seems like a foolish thing to do if you're expecting the world to end," Talmadge mumbled under his breath.

A minute later, he heard Papa and Dwight hit the front porch running.

"Dust storm's coming," Papa said as they came through the door. "Mr. Weatherby—the overseer—drove over to tell us. He heared it on the radio."

"Dust storm?" Mama said in a puzzled voice. "In swampland?"

"Oklahoma dust," Papa said. "I want everybody in the front room. Alvira, I'll need a quilt to cover the west window. Talmadge, get me two hammers and a handful of short nails."

"Yes, sir." When he ran into the kitchen, Jasper was whining outside the back door. Talmadge let him in, then went to the corner where Papa kept his big tool chest, his most precious possession. He opened the top of the chest, and the blended aroma of wood and steel and the oil Papa rubbed on his tools floated into his nostrils.

Papa and Dwight were already holding the quilt up to the window when he went into the front room and gave them the hammers and nails. Papa began putting nails through the quilt above the window because Dwight was not tall enough to reach that high. Dwight put in nails at the bottom, then they started on the sides.

"You know how hard it is to make a quilt?" Mama said.

"I'm sorry, Mother," Papa said. "But we can't chance glass flying around in here."

You could hear the wind coming now. Talmadge, with Missy behind him, ran to the kitchen and looked through that window. The approaching dust, a cloud connecting earth and sky, wrapped around trees, swallowed them.

"Get in here!" Papa called.

When they reached the front room, Annabelle, the mouser Mr. Williams had given Roseanne, was mewing and rubbing against her legs. She picked the cat up. It worried Talmadge. Roseanne had never liked cats until Mr. Williams gave her this one, which could be a sign that she was sweet on Mr. Williams. At the place in Mississippi, Papa had come near to putting a bullet hole through a man who tried to court her.

"Stand with your backs against the wall," Papa said.

The wind hit, wailed as it rounded the corners. Dirt and twigs and leaves beat against the window and the side of the house. Something thumped on the roof. The quilt billowed, yet there didn't seem to be enough air in the room. Talmadge sat down on the floor. He might as well be comfortable.

"Papa," Missy said, "Talmadge ain't doing his part to hold up the wall."

Dwight and Papa laughed, and Dwight hugged Missy. Dwight looked like his old self right now, his face tender for Missy, excitement sparking out from him because of the storm. Mama didn't even smile. Roseanne's eyes were closed and her lips moved in silent prayer.

Silence came suddenly and completely.

Roseanne opened her eyes. "Is it over?" she asked

scarcely above a whisper.

"It's over," Papa said.

They went out on the front porch. The trees that had been bright with spring-newness were half-naked. Fully bloomed jonquils, the one thing that had pleased Mama about this house, bent low to the ground under a coating of dust.

Tears came into Roseanne's eyes and Mama's face twisted. Talmadge thought she was going to cry, and he wished she would. When he was small, Mama had cried sometimes about the bitterness between her and Papa's families. But she had not cried when they lost their place in Wild Hog Holler, and she hadn't cried since. It would probably help her if she did. When they lived in Mississippi, anger had built up inside him. Finally he had cried long into the night, and the next morning the anger was gone.

Missy took Mama's hand. "The flowers will be all right, Mama. I'll bring out a pan of water and wash them so they can stand up again."

Mama's mouth trembled, then thinned into a hard line. She pulled her hand away from Missy's and went inside.

Chapter 6

"You open a drawer and there's dust in it," Peadod said.

Talmadge, walking beside him on the way to school, sighed. A week had passed since the storm and it was still all Peadod talked about. "Miss Gibson's apt to give us a spelling test today," Talmadge said. "I remember all the words. You want me to go over them with you?"

Peadod shrugged. "No matter how much I study, I can't get them right. 'Course, Mr. Wilson—Stinky's dad— says it wasn't really a storm, that it was just a March wind that picked up a handful of Oklahoma dust. Stinky used to live in Oklahoma." He looked across the road to the left at the Limon pasture. "It got the

Dolens. They're moving off."

Talmadge's interest rose.

"Mrs. Dolen ain't been well. Mama says she had a kind of nervous breakdown some time back and the dust was the last straw. Mama says she reckons the Dolens will ship their belongings on a freight and take a passenger back up to where Mrs. Dolen's folks live in Missouri."

A rent acreage was available! Other families who had been here longer than the McLinns would want the acreage, but who could get it without going deep into debt? To rent, you had to have your own mules and equipment. The McLinns hadn't spent any of the cash they received in Wild Hog Holler for their stock and farming equipment. Also, with Papa and Dwight both working at the place in Mississippi, all of them but Missy picking cotton, and Mama being so frugal.... He told himself to act calm and not let his excitement show.

He and Peadod rounded the corner; now they were on the road that went past the post office and the store. "Where's the Dolens' acreage?"

"On Gumbo Ridge, about a half mile the other side of the highway and the track."

Talmadge chewed his bottom lip. Prices were up some. Mules were expensive, and it took a lot of equipment to grow cotton. They would need to buy Mr. Dolen's plows, his harrow and disk, his wagon. He and Peadod turned the corner; they were passing the post office when a black car drove away from the store, came out onto the road. Gathering speed, the car came toward them. As it passed, the driver, who was wearing a hat and a suit, lifted his hand in greeting. Peadod waved back. Talmadge turned around, watched the car round the corner onto the main road.

"That was Dr. Spain," Peadod said. "He lives in Riverton, which is four miles south. His office is there, too, but he takes care of everybody on Limon, and everybody in between here and Riverton."

"Who's sick?"

"Maybe nobody. Maybe some lady had a baby. After he makes his visit, Dr. Spain goes to the store to see if any telephone calls have come in for him."

They were beyond the bayou and passing the white houses. Talmadge suddenly stopped walking. The truck! Last night after supper, Papa had asked Mama to put on her coat and go for a walk with him. If Papa sold them the truck, the Dolens wouldn't have to ship their belongings on a freight train, and the McLinns would have even more cash.

"It don't make much sense to wait until we're almost there to decide you ain't going," Peadod said.

Talmadge laughed and started walking again. He still had not been really accepted at school, and Peadod was not much more popular than he. Getting a rent acreage would mean a lot. The others would see him differently when he no longer lived on the Newground.

Chapter 7

When Talmadge stopped at the post office that afternoon, Miss Hettie handed him two letters. The one from Cousin Maybelle was addressed to both Mama and Papa. The other one, addressed only to Mama, was from Grandpa Thornton.

Jasper trotted to meet him as he turned into his yard. "I bet you're glad as me to see this nice weather," Talmadge said. When he went inside, Mama was in the front room. He handed her the letters. "You hit the jackpot."

Gazing at the top envelope, she moved her lips the way Papa did when he read silently. "Maybelle's mighty faithful," she said. She looked at the other envelope a long time, then lay both letters on the sewing machine.

And there, Talmadge knew, they would stay until Papa read them aloud to everybody tonight. How could she wait like that? If he ever got a letter, he would read it immediately. And it was bound to make Papa feel bad when he read letters from Grandpa Thornton. "Tell your husband I thank him," was the only reference he ever made to Papa. Once Talmadge had asked Papa what Grandpa Thornton thanked him for, and Papa had answered, "I reckon I'd as soon not tell you." That meant don't ask again. Maybe Papa hadn't shot a Thornton when he had the chance. Talmadge started toward his room, turned around. "Mama, can I go crawfishing tomorrow morning with Peadod?"

"You clean your room and pump me a barrel of wash water, you can." She gazed through the window a moment, shook herself, and went into the kitchen.

Sitting on the front porch with his feet on the top step, Talmadge looked down the road. Peadod was late. He had said he would be here around eight and it was almost eight-thirty. Papa and Dwight had left for work hours ago. But they only had to work until noon on Saturday.

Mama had been quiet through supper last night. She hadn't said anything after Papa read the letters, neither of which was very long or said anything important. This morning, her mind seemed to be somewhere else.

The screen door opened and he glanced over his shoulder. Roseanne was coming out on the porch. "You mind if I sit with you while you're waiting?" she asked.

Talmadge smiled at her. "I'd be honored you'd sit with me. I bet there ain't a boy in my class has a big sister pretty as you." She seemed to have gotten even prettier since they had moved here.

Roseanne tweaked his hair, then sat down and smoothed her skirt over her knees.

They sat without talking. It made him a little uncomfortable because he was by nature a talker. He knew, though, that Roseanne was content to sit in silence. Sometimes he went for days without really noticing her. She was Mama's helper. She worked quietly, without complaint or comment.

"Your friends are coming," Roseanne said.

Friends? She was right. Two boys were coming. John Edward was with Peadod. "John Edward's the smartest boy in the class," he said. "I admire him, but I don't really consider him a friend. Peadod can drive you crazy, but I reckon he is."

"Smart people need friends, too," Roseanne said as she rose to leave.

"You don't have to go. Stay and meet them."

She gave a slight smile. "I see Peadod at church."

Since the church was not Methodist, none of the rest

of the family went. Mama had made it clear that she disapproved of Roseanne's going. Roseanne hadn't argued with her; she just kept going.

"And I've run into John Edward on the road," Roseanne said. "I'm going to sit under my tree a while."

Her tree was a fair-sized hickory, and since it was her dreaming place, he never went too close to it when he looked for firewood. Even if she weren't there, it would be like invading her privacy.

As she rounded the porch corner, he heard Annabelle meow and knew she had come from under the house and was following Roseanne.

He picked up his fishing pole and his bait—small chunks of side meat—called to Mama that he was leaving, and walked up the road to meet Peadod and John Edward.

"I seen your sister on the porch with you," Peadod said. "She sure is pretty. Mr. Williams thinks so, too. When they sit together at church, he has a hard time taking his eyes off her to look at the preacher."

Talmadge frowned. Mr. Williams might not have a reputation as a woman-user like the man in Mississippi that Papa had threatened to shoot if he didn't stay away from Roseanne, but Mr. Williams had two children. Papa wouldn't like it if something was going on between Roseanne and Mr. Williams. So they sat together at church and Roseanne liked the cat he had given to her. That didn't mean anything. Mr. Williams hadn't walked her home. It was nothing serious.

As they passed his yard, John Edward kept looking at the green jars. Talmadge was so used to them he hardly noticed them ordinarily, but now they seemed to jump at him. He gave an embarrassed laugh. "They came down to Mama from her great aunt. They're supposed to have a magical power or something to keep evil spirits away."

"Belief in the supernatural is an interesting phenomenon," John Edward said.

Jasper ranged ahead of them as they walked toward the canal. When they were there and had settled at Peadod's favorite spot, Talmadge tied a piece of the side meat on his line and dropped it into the water. Moments later, the line tightened. He slowly lifted his fishing pole, and stared at a big red crawfish with its claws clamped around the chunk of fat. Talmadge had crawfished before, but he had never caught one that big. Mostly he had caught small gray crawfish.

"He's a beauty," John Edward said.

Between pulling in crawfish, they talked. John Edward told how he hoped to be a teacher, and Peadod said he wanted to do something to help people.

"You do that already," John Edward said. "You're kind-hearted. How about you, Talmadge? What's your dream?"

He could hardly tell them that he didn't go beyond dreaming that the McLinns would stay on in Limon, and that he would have a lot of friends. "I don't know yet." He thought about Dr. Spain passing him now and then in his black car. "A doctor, maybe."

"You'd be a good one," John Edward said.

They sang "New River Train" and "Down in the Valley" and one of Mr. Whitis's favorites, "The Quilting Party."

"We ought to be on the radio," Peadod said.

"We're good all right," Talmadge said solemnly, and John Edward laughed so hard he lost a crawfish.

"According to the sun, it's getting on toward noon," Talmadge said. "We better go."

"We sure had," Peadod said. "Mama makes a good dinner on Saturday. I don't want to miss it."

At his house, Talmadge said good-bye to them and hurried around to the back. Papa was already home. Talmadge didn't know how he knew that at first, then he realized that he heard Papa whistling. Papa whistling? He couldn't remember the last time he had heard Papa whistling.

Papa, standing on the back steps, looked into Talmadge's bucket. "Ain't nothing better than fried crawdad tails," he said.

He was not just happy about something; he was excited.

"Soon's you wash up, come on inside," Papa said.

Talmadge washed his hands at the pump and all but ran inside and into the front room. The others were already there.

Papa cleared his throat and looked around at them. "We'uns," he said, "have got ourselves a rent acreage right here on Limon."

Missy clapped and squealed. She didn't really understand the significance of what Papa had told them, Talmadge thought. She only knew that Papa was happy. Roseanne's mouth curved in a slight smile.

Mama gazed down at the floor, her face still. Dwight's "angry-with-the-world" expression etched itself a little deeper into his face. Dwight hadn't always been like this. It had begun when he failed third grade. When they moved to Mississippi and he quit school to work, the anger had grown.

As for Talmadge, he wanted to shout for joy. He would no longer live on the Newground. His status at school was about to change.

Chapter 8

Talmadge leaned against the kitchen table. "What do you think, Mama? How do you like the house?"

Putting dishes in the cabinet, she answered without looking at him. "It's got its merits. And it's nice to have a cow. But with the truck gone...."

Talmadge clamped his teeth together and closed his eyes from frustration with her. She still had it in her mind that they would eventually go back to Rim County. He wanted to tell her that from the morning they had driven away, Papa had never looked back, never been homesick for Wild Hog Holler.

In a flat voice, Mama said, "We had to give Mr. Dolen

ever bit of our cash. But that weren't enough to pay for his stock and cotton wagon and farming equipment. Dwight put in some of his savings, and we went into debt to Mr. Limon."

"But Mama, we got a good house and a nice barn. And opportunity."

As if she hadn't heard him, she said, "Since your daddy ain't working by the day, we'll have to borrow scrip to buy our staples from now through harvest. When the cotton's sold next winter and we pay our debt, at ten percent interest, there'll likely be just enough money left over to buy seed for next year's crop."

She was purposely looking on the dark side, Talmadge thought. And she ought to at least appreciate the house. The big kitchen had linoleum on the floor. The front room accommodated Mama and Papa's bed, the chifforobe, and the sewing machine without even looking crowded. His and Dwight's room, which had been added on behind part of the kitchen, was the smallest room in the whole house. But he wasn't complaining.

They had shade trees, a barn and a lot, and even a pasture. Papa said Goliath and Penny might not be the most handsome pair of mules he'd ever seen, but they were young and healthy. They had a Poland China sow and a cow, and the Plymouth Rock chickens they had brought from the Newground.

The McLinns had good neighbors, too. The Clarks,

who sharecropped ten acres of the McLinns' rent land, lived not far yonder side of the ditch. Mrs. Clark had brought Mama a quart of blackberries. The Teasleys lived in a two-story house by the track and Mrs. Teasley had brought a cake right after the McLinns moved in. When Mama told Mrs. Teasley she didn't care for the Plymouth Rocks, that she preferred Golden Buff Minorcas, Mrs. Teasley had said she wouldn't have anything but Golden Buffs and had taken to Mama.

Mama picked up one of the green jars and, her face tight, put it on the top cabinet shelf.

Talmadge's mouth sagged open.

"I can't put them where they ought to be," Mama said. "It comes natural to young'uns to throw rocks."

He checked a grin. The gravel road afforded an advantage he hadn't thought about. The embarrassing jars would not be out there for people to see.

When Mama had put all the jars in the cabinet, she stepped to the open-front wooden counter attached to the wall at the end of the cookstove and rinsed her cloth in the dishpan. Talmadge gazed at her back. She was twice the size of Miss Gibson. Her homemade print dress was faded. And she was barefoot. He had considered asking John Edward and Peadod to come over this Saturday to see the house, but it would be embarrassing to introduce John Edward to Mama. It was wrong to be thinking this way; he was ashamed of himself.

"I washed down the privy seat with lye water and rinsed it good," he said. "Is there anything else you want me to do?"

She hung the cloth on a nail in the wall. "Not that I can think of."

"Then can I go down to the ditch that runs through Gumbo Ridge? It's not very far, a little west...."

"I seen it. Ugly water that runs through a culvert under the road. Go on." Without turning to look at him, she went out on the back porch. He would think she was crying, except Mama never cried. But she was surely thinking about the stream that ran through Wild Hog Holler, its water so clear you could count the rocks in the bed.

At the ditch, Talmadge walked a narrow path along the shelf. He was no longer on Limon; the gravel road marked its northern boundary, but nobody here paid any attention to boundaries. To his left, well below him, ran a twelve-foot-wide stream of sluggish water. To his right, beyond the shelf, a mound of soil that had been scooped out to make the ditch was covered with bushes, more weeds, and small trees.

As he walked, Talmadge constantly moved his eyes over the weeds and vines ahead of him on both sides of the footpath. In Mississippi, he had learned to keep a lookout for two very poisonous creatures. Black widow spiders were most likely to be in woodpiles, and cottonmouth moccasins were apt to be in or near water. You had to be careful not to come close enough to a moccasin that it felt threatened.

Within a short time, he came upon a circle of sweet clover the size of a small room. "I knew I'd find it," he murmured. "I got myself a dreaming place."

He laid down on his back and put his hands beneath his head. Somewhere nearby a meadowlark was singing. If he could duplicate those pure, sweet notes on his harmonica, he would have something. Lazy white clouds drifted across a milky blue sky. "I got one more request, Lord," he said. "I want to be accepted at school." He turned over on his stomach. The Lord could read his mind, but it wouldn't be like he was asking in prayer. He wanted more than acceptance. He wanted to be kind of popular.

Chapter 9

Yesterday's brief downpour had washed the April sky. The sun had quickly dried the land, and the scent of flowers floated on a light breeze. Behind the school after lunch, Talmadge stood at the fringe of onlookers, including some girls, watching a marble game.

Most of the boys used either a good cat's-eye or an agate for a shooter. Stinky's shooter was a white agate. A seventh-grade boy was using a steely. Talmadge didn't like steelies. They could chip marbles, or break them. But he liked the way they played here. At the Mississippi school, you shot each time from the edge of a large circle. In this game, the target marbles were placed inside a small oval. If your shootin' taw didn't stop for ten feet after it went through the oval, you had to shoot from there. This game took skill. You might have a good shooter, but if you couldn't put English on it, you didn't stand a chance.

Marbles was a game he could play, but nobody had asked him. Some of the others besides Peadod and John Edward did smile at him sometimes. Meg Weston had even told him she and her friends had fidgeted and looked away when he came around because they were ashamed that they had yelled at him to go back to Wild Hog Holler when he and Stinky had the fight.

The marble game ended just before the bell rang to mark the end of lunch hour. Talmadge walked away. Peadod was not with him because he had been in the game, and he and the others were talking, laughing, replaying it.

"Hey, Hillbilly," Stinky called.

Talmadge ignored the call.

Stinky caught up with him. "You know how to play marbles, Hillbilly?"

Talmadge stopped walking and faced him. "Yes," he said. In a low, challenging voice, he added, "I can play right well."

Shaking his fingers, Stinky said, "Ooh, you hear that? Hillbilly can play right well."

There was laughter, but Talmadge thought some of it was uncomfortable laughter. And LaVerne said,

"Ambrose, you make me want to puke."

Stinky flushed, but he didn't answer LaVerne. His eyes narrowed, and he said to Talmadge, "Tomorrow, after lunch. Just you and me."

Talmadge nodded. He didn't trust himself to speak. He might sound too eager, or he might sound nervous. He wanted to play, but he was afraid he would lose.

By the time he reached home that afternoon, his nervousness had grown. He had to win tomorrow.

Jasper, sleeping on the front porch, roused himself and came down the steps to meet him. "How you doing, boy?" Talmadge said. "You ought to be thankful you're a dog. You don't have worries like people do."

Mama and Roseanne were working in the garden plot to the left of the yard. Missy wasn't with them. She was probably down the road at Betty Ann's house. That was the one thing he missed about living on the New-ground. There, Missy had always run to greet him in the afternoon. They had scarcely moved here when she had discovered Betty Ann. Now, either Betty Ann was here or Missy was at Betty Ann's.

Talmadge stopped in the kitchen, took a handful of cookies from the jar. He started to take them to his room, but changed his mind. He might drop crumbs and Mama and Dwight would both get on him. He ate the cookies, went to his room, opened his top drawer, and took out a tobacco sack bulging with marbles.

He loosened the drawstring, poured some of the

marbles into his hand. He had some pretty ones, and his shootin' taw, an especially fine variegated red and clear, had done well by him.

He put all the marbles back in the sack except for the red and clear. That one he set on top of the chest of drawers. It might not stand up against Stinky's agate. It surely wouldn't draw much admiration. But he knew of a marble that would. He pictured it in the bottom drawer, Dwight's keepsake drawer. A single blue agate inside a small leather pouch. Mr. Parks had given Dwight the agate for his eleventh birthday.

Talmadge got down on his knees and grasped the drawer knobs. He let them go without pulling. Every time he opened that drawer he worried that Dwight might walk in and catch him.

There was no danger of Dwight's coming in now. Either he or Papa was plowing. The other one was digging up Johnson grass and putting it in a tow sack. When the grass dried, Papa would burn it.

Dwight hardly ever opened that drawer anymore. There was nothing in it except keepsakes—a softball glove, a stuffed bear Dwight had won at a carnival, old funny books, drawings. Dwight used to draw a lot, mostly pictures of machines, including some he dreamed up.

Talmadge rubbed his palms on his thighs, noted exactly how tightly the drawer was closed, and pulled it open. He ran his hand down in the right back corner and took out the leather pouch. His fingers trembled when he removed the agate. He put the pouch back where it had been, closed the drawer, and went to the south window, the agate cradled in his palm.

He had never seen a marble that compared with this one. It looked like a jewel, a clear blue jewel that made you want to cry. Dwight would kill him if he even knew he was fooling with it. If Dwight were the right kind of brother, he would give it to him. Dwight didn't play marbles anymore; he hadn't so much as looked at this agate for a couple of years. It was sinful to let a marble like this sit in a drawer.

Talmadge went outside, placed some cat's-eyes on smooth ground, and shot the agate. It was as if it were alive, and glad to be out of the pouch. He shot from close up and far back, from straight on and from difficult angles. This was a marble you could talk to, a marble you could put English on.

He gathered up his own marbles, put them in the tobacco sack. Carefully, he laid the blue on top of them. After tomorrow he would never touch it again. He imagined a lot of people standing around watching the game. He imagined them clapping when he won.

Chapter 10

From the time the weather had warmed, students had gone outside to eat lunch. Sitting on the grass behind the school with Peadod and John Edward, Talmadge ate his bologna and biscuit sandwich. He wished he could relax, stop thinking about the upcoming marble game with Stinky.

Peadod took a bite of his sandwich, which was also bologna, but he had light bread instead of a biscuit. "I ain't ever seen a prettier agate than your blue," he said.

"I just hope you don't lose it," John Edward said. "Stinky's good."

"I'm good, too," Talmadge said. That wasn't bragging. It was the truth.

When they had finished their sandwiches, they went to the grassless area behind the school and waited until the others came. Stinky looked straight at Talmadge and smirked. Pretending that he hadn't noticed, Talmadge watched John Edward draw the squashed oval in the dirt. Talmadge and Stinky put four marbles each in it. John Edward drew the taw line, laid down the sharp-pointed stick, and put his hands behind his back.

"Two," Talmadge said.

"Five," Stinky said.

John Edward took his hands from behind his back and held up four fingers. Stinky had the first shot. Talmadge managed to hide his irritation when Stinky brought out a steely to use as his shooter. But if Stinky wanted to chance chipping marbles he won, that was his business.

Stinky took his position, put his knuckles on the taw line, and shot. One of Talmadge's cat's-eyes bounced out. The steely came to a stop six inches from the edge of the oval. That was one of the advantages of a steely; it didn't travel once it hit the target.

Turning the blue between his thumb and forefinger, Talmadge heard murmurs of admiration for the agate. He shot and one of Stinky's marbles spun out. Too hard. His taw was a good three feet outside. He'd have to ease up, remember that the blue had wings like an angel.

The second round came and went and he and Stinky were even up. He had eight of Stinky's marbles; Stinky had eight of his.

They were nearing the end of the third—and last—round. Two marbles were left in the oval—both Stinky's. But Talmadge had a good position. He drew a line with his eyes. He could take them both. Ricochet off the first marble, then tap the other one. He shot; the first marble spun out.

He heard an intake of breath around him, knew the same thing they did. The agate, already slowed by the first marble, was going to hit the second one dead center. Stinky's marble rolled straight ahead and out. But the solid hit had slowed the blue down too much. Make it, please make it out, Talmadge silently pleaded. His agate stopped just inside the line. He almost sagged forward. All Stinky had to do was send the steely in at a slow roll and he would have Dwight's agate.

Feet moved, but nobody left. It was over, Talmadge thought dully; they might as well leave.

Stinky took his time, rolling the steely between his palms, tilting his head this way and that. He was about to shoot. The feet stopped moving; nobody made a sound. In the instant Stinky put his knuckles on the ground, Talmadge knew the glitter in his eyes was for something more than anticipated victory.

Stinky licked his lips—and sent the steely across the ground like a bullet.

Talmadge's whole body jerked with the low-pitched, vibrating sound of steel hitting glass. Dimly, as if he were far away, he heard a gasp go through the watching crowd, blending with the squealing and laughter from the side yard. The moment passed as the agate bounced into the air, landed, rolled a short way and stopped. It was still in one piece, but from the way it had rolled, it was damaged.

He felt the same way he had the day Stinky grabbed his book and threw it on the ground. He wanted to hit Stinky, hit him again and again. The combination of the bell ringing and Stinky himself saved him.

"You can keep your shootin' taw," Stinky said as he loped around and picked up the steely.

His insides shaking, Talmadge stood up. "You won it square."

"Nah," Stinky said. "I got my sweetheart." He kissed the steely.

For a pulse beat, when Peadod brought him the agate and dropped it in his palm, Talmadge thought he had been wrong, that it was all right. Then he saw the crack running through it and quickly dropped it in his pocket.

The girls standing on the fringes were sending him looks of sympathy. LaVerne blew him a kiss off her fingers. Paul, a quiet boy who hung around with Stinky's bunch, touched his arm and said, "Good game." Boys who had never had the time of day for him clapped him on the back. They were letting him know they didn't approve of the way Stinky had made the last shot.

No, there was more to it than that. As they started down the hall toward their classroom, boys slowed their step to walk with him. It had happened. He was one of them. But he was too miserable to enjoy it.

Jasper came out from under the house, across the yard and up the road to meet him. Ordinarily he would say, "Sure is nice of you to stir your lazy bones and come to meet me." Today he got down on his knees and hugged Jasper.

As he turned into the yard, he saw Mama working in the garden plot. He went up the steps, crossed the porch, and blinked to adjust his eyes to the dimness as he opened the screen door and went inside. The house smelled of steam rising from damp, clean clothes. He knew before he reached the kitchen that Roseanne was ironing. And Missy was telling her about playing house with Betty Ann.

"Hi," he said as he went through the kitchen toward his room.

"What's wrong?" Missy asked.

"Nothing's wrong," Talmadge said. "I'm just tired."

Roseanne set the flat iron on the end of the board. "Did something happen at school?"

"No! I told y'all. I'm just tired." He went into his

room and shut the door. He waited until he heard Roseanne and Missy talking, then slipped open Dwight's
drawer and took out the pouch.

Dwight hadn't opened that drawer for a long time,
but what if he did? What if he picked up the pouch
and took out the agate? But if he opened the drawer
and the pouch wasn't there for him to see, maybe he
wouldn't think about it.

Talmadge put the agate in the pouch and laid it on
the floor. Quietly, he closed the drawer. He changed
into his old, too-short overalls, and put the pouch in a
side pocket. He would have to go through the kitchen
again. This room didn't have an outside door.

He didn't look at Missy and Roseanne as he crossed
the kitchen. "I'm going down to the ditch bank for a
few minutes." They already knew he was upset. They
would just think he was going to his special spot.

At the ditch bank, he walked across his dreaming
place, where sweet clover and short grass grew, and
pulled up a cocklebur a few feet beyond it. On his
knees, he scooped out the loose dirt where the cocklebur roots had been. He opened his pocketknife, loosened more dirt, and scooped it out. Then he buried
the pouch and the beautiful blue.

Chapter 11

almadge laughed as other boys shoved each other to sit by him at the last morning assembly before school let out for summer. Things had really changed for him in the six weeks since the marble game. That afternoon when he got off the bus, he waved until it was a blur in the distance. He wouldn't see his friends who lived up the highway until school started again.

At the top of the railroad bed he stopped and stood for a moment between the main track and the switch track, which started a hundred yards north of the road and stretched southward past a boarded-up depot that had served during sawmilling days. "I'm king of the

69

hill," he murmured, and laughed at himself.

As he walked toward home, the gravel made a crunching sound under his shoes. Birds sang. Somewhere in the distance a dog barked. He took out his harmonica and played a made-up tune to go with the sounds. He had no worries. Once Dwight had asked him if he had gotten to play in any marble games at school. It had scared Talmadge, but he had managed to shrug and say, "A few," as if it were not important. Dwight hadn't said anything more, so he had evidently just been making conversation.

He had passed the Clarks' house and was almost to the ditch when he saw Dr. Spain's car coming. Now it was passing the McLinns' house. He put his harmonica in his pocket and moved to the side of the road. Dr. Spain lifted his hand in greeting as he passed, and Talmadge waved. The day he had told Peadod and John Edward he wanted to be a doctor, he had only said it because he hadn't considered his future. But the notion that he would become a doctor no longer seemed so far-fetched.

The house seemed to be waiting for him, and Mama's big porch rocker looked as if it were holding out its arms. Annabelle was dozing in the rocker. Since it was hot today, Jasper would be waiting in the deep shade under the porch.

Just before he reached the path that led from the road to the house, Jasper trotted up to him. "How you doing, boy?" Talmadge said. He and Jasper were half-way up the path when Annabelle yawned and stretched, then dived feet first off the rocker to the porch and came to brush against his legs. Laughing, he said, "What you two going to do tomorrow afternoon? School let out for summer today, you know."

"Anybody home?" he called as he went inside. He hoped they were all here; he wanted to show them his report card. Except for one B, he had made A's this month.

"Just me," Mama said. "In the kitchen."

She was folding clothes, but when he held out his report card, she stopped working, took the card, and and studied it front and back.

"It ain't only writ on the card," she said as she handed it back to him. "It's writ all over your face. You got a right to be proud. Far as I know, ain't no McLinn afore you ever made it through sixth grade." She took a towel from the basket and folded it. "I understand you wanted to go longer than Dwight or your daddy did. And I can see you've got to liking school now that you got friends. But too much schooling makes a body dissatisfied with their lot. I seen it happen more than once." She looked straight into his eyes. "It's time you pulled your own weight."

Talmadge thought he might be sick. She was telling him, telling him now so he would have all summer to adjust, that he couldn't go to school next year.

"Soon's you change and have a bite to eat, get your hoe and head for the cornfield to help Dwight and Roseanne with the weeding." She sighed. "Come Monday, we'll be thinning cotton. The first chopping."

"Mama, about school, please, you got to listen...."

"I've been listening. And seeing. Now go on. I don't want to hear no more about it."

As he went toward his room, Missy came in from the back porch and he knew from her face that she had heard everything. She followed him into his room and put her arms around his waist. "I was countin' on you being there when I start to school next year," she said.

"She'll change her mind before then."

Missy shook her head. "Mama don't ever change her mind."

Chapter 12

The days went by in a blur of chopping cotton and blazing sun. There was little rain, but Mr. Teasley told Papa not to worry, that cotton was a drought-resistant crop.

The cotton, though, was not their only concern. To keep it from dropping to four cents a pound, as it had in 1932, the government had made a rule that only so much cotton could be planted. If a farmer overplanted cotton in his acreage, he had to plow it up. So they not only had the usual cornfield, vegetable garden, Irish potato, sweet potato, watermelon, and cantaloupe patches, they also had peanuts.

Between cultivation, scanty rains, and hand-toted

water, the fruit and vegetable patches did well. But in the small, untilled and unwatered pasture, the shallow-rooted grass died and the earth cracked.

The cotton was laid by early, just past the middle of June. The hot, dry weather continued, and Talmadge worried about the creatures in general and the chicks in particular. Back in the spring, Mrs. Teasley had brought Mama a dozen Golden Buff Minorca chicks, all female except for one cocky little rooster. Mama had kept them on layers of newspapers behind a low board barricade until they feathered out and could move fast enough to save themselves from a diving hawk. Papa had built a pen and a shelter outside to keep them separated from the Plymouth Rocks, which Mama was cooking one by one.

Now in the early stage of being pullets, the Minorcas panted in the afternoon heat.

Talmadge and the others seemed to be constantly pumping troughs of water, and they poured water in the lot to make cooling wallows for the pigs. Honeysuckle lay chewing her cud; her male calf walked slowly instead of frisking about. Goliath and Penny stood side by side, facing opposite directions, either in the barn shade or beneath the persimmon tree in the pasture, and switched their tails to brush the flies off each other's faces.

At night, Talmadge would toss and turn for a while, then get out of bed and go out on the back porch and sit with his legs dangling over the edge. Sometimes mosquitoes sucked his blood and left itching welts, but when a breeze touched him, he savored it, and thought about the coming of autumn. He could talk to Papa about going to school, but he didn't want to do that. This was between Mama and him.

After breakfast on a July Saturday morning, he walked up to the store, stopping sometimes to look at the cotton fields, now in full bloom and beautiful. Peadod and John Edward were at the store, sipping grape Nehis. Talmadge bought an Orange Crush and they took their drinks outside to sit beneath a shade tree on the bayou bank. Peadod and John Edward told stories about the heat, and Peadod said that in the big Limon pasture a heifer had stepped in an earth crack and broken her leg.

Talmadge, thinking about Mama's saying he couldn't go to school this year, didn't tell them that in their dried-up, never-tilled pasture, some of the cracks were six inches wide. He sat silently, and finally John Edward asked, "What's wrong, Talmadge?"

"Just tired," he said. "I didn't sleep good last night."

"You're not worried about the rumor that Mr. Limon is going to tractors next year, are you?" John Edward asked. "If he does, it's more likely to affect day hands and sharecroppers than it is renters."

Talmadge shook his head. "No, I'm not worried about that."

"What you ain't worried about?" LeRoy dropped down beside him.

Talmadge and the others greeted LeRoy, then John Edward looked from Talmadge to LeRoy and back again. "Two minutes have passed and neither of you have reached for your harmonicas."

"I was waiting on old sober-face here," LeRoy said.

LeRoy played as fine a harmonica as Talmadge had ever heard and, ordinarily, he would quickly lose himself in their music, the improvising, the notes that came from some magical, hidden source. But today, he couldn't play. He stood and said, "I better go before it gets any hotter."

By the time he passed the ditch, every step was an effort. His clubfoot felt as if it weighed twenty pounds, and he didn't really want to go home at all. So far, he had been able to say no more about school, but it had been hard.

As he turned into the yard, Jasper walked slowly to greet him. When Talmadge went up the steps, Jasper went back under the house. Talmadge crossed the porch, opened the screen door, and blinked to adjust his eyes to the inside dimness.

Mama, sitting in her front-room rocker hemming a dress for Missy, was the only one there. Dwight, she told him, had gone to Riverton. Roseanne, who had been going on Saturday afternoons to stay with Mr. Williams' children, had decided that she would go this morning instead, and make dinner for the Williamses. Missy was at Betty Ann's, and Papa was at the Clarks'.

Only Talmadge and Mama were here. This was his chance to talk with her about school, to make her understand. He took a deep breath. "Mama, about school.... The reason I want to go so bad is that I want to make something of my life."

She didn't look up from her sewing. "You saying your daddy hasn't made nothing of his? You remember, we had a nice farm. It got took away from us, yes, but it wasn't because he didn't have enough schooling. You know Mr. Clark?"

Talmadge waited. She wasn't really asking; she was aware that he knew all the Clarks down to the baby.

"Well, he went up through eighth grade. And look what he's doing now. Sharecropping."

"It's not just for a good job I want to go to school. It's the learning, it's.... Can't you see what I'm talking about?"

"I see more'n you think I do," she said with a bitter harshness. "You like getting inside books so you don't have to face the fact of how hard life is. And since you got friends at school now, you want to be with them. Now go on. I don't want to talk about it no more."

Quietly, Talmadge said, "Yes, ma'am."

Her head snapped up; he saw the surprise in her face. He sent a thought to her: it's not over. Then he turned and left the room.

"It may be temporary," Papa said at breakfast a few days later, "but it's cooled off some."

"Yeah," Dwight said in a wry voice. "I bet it don't get any higher than ninety-five today."

Roseanne laughed. Mama said, "It'll be a hundred and fifty in here whilst we're canning pole beans." Roseanne stopped laughing and closed her eyes.

By eight o'clock, Papa was gone, taking advantage of the pleasant morning to go to the store for the flour, cornmeal, and sugar Mama needed. Dwight and Talmadge helped pick and string the beans. When the canning began, Dwight went to his room to lie down and read. Betty Ann had come to see Missy; now they were leaving, going to Betty Ann's.

Talmadge decided to go outside. As he went down the back steps, he glanced over at the Minorcas' pen. They weren't lolling around today; the cooler weather had made them restless. Their water pan was almost full. Mama had assigned Missy the task of keeping it filled, and she had been very responsible.

He went to the side yard, stretched out beneath the hickory, and daydreamed that he was at school, that it was the first day of seventh grade. He and his friends were talking and laughing as they went into their class-room. There were people in the room, but somebody he expected to be there wasn't. His eyes flew open. There had been something wrong about the chicken pen! He scrambled to his feet, ran back to it, counted. One of the chicks was missing. The gate was closed now, but Missy must have left it ajar when she took the water into the pen.

He went to the road and looked up and down. Even though they kept a bowl of gravel in the pen, all that gravel in the road might have enticed the stray. He checked under the house, went to the backyard again and looked beyond the lot and barn to the pasture. He knew; he thought he had known all along. He went to the pasture, stopped beside an earth crack, listened, and walked again. At the next one, a muffled sound disturbed the stillness.

He lay down, heard panting and fluttering, as if the little pullet were trying to climb or fly out to the light above it. The crack surely narrowed as it deepened. Lying on his side, he ran his arm into the crack, but after a moment, he knew it was hopeless. He withdrew his arm and stood. He couldn't leave the chick there to suffer; he would go get Dwight.

Go get Dwight? Depend on his big brother to do what had to be done? He went as quickly as he could to the toolshed, and got the shovel.

Even after the fluttering and panting stopped, he continued to strike the hard ground and push in dirt; he tasted salty dirt and knew he was crying. Nobody should have to live like this. He was not going to spend his life chopping and picking cotton and shoveling dirt in on live chickens.

When he had put the shovel back in the shed, he washed his face and hands at the pump and went into the house. Standing in the steamy kitchen, he said to Mama in a flat voice, "One of your pullets got out of the pen and fell into a crack. I buried it alive."

Roseanne gave a little cry. Mama's face twisted, then she said, "You done the only thing there was to do."

As if she had not reacted, he said with the same toneless voice, "I am going to school. You can't stop me."

For a heartbeat, there was no sound, no movement. Then Mama yelled, "Get out of here! Get out of my kitchen!"

Chapter 13

Talmadge walked out of the kitchen, across the porch, and down the back steps.

Before he reached the front porch, he crawled under the house, drew up his knees, folded his arms across them, and laid his forehead on his arms. Jasper came, whined, and lay down beside him. At a faint, out-of-place sound, a brushing against the earth, he lifted his head and saw Roseanne's skirt and legs. Her faded blue skirt had small orange flowers sprinkled over it; her legs and feet were brown as dried berries.

Bending from the waist, she peered at him. Her blouse clung to her skin; she was flushed from the canning heat and her sun-streaked hair hung in damp strands. "Since I'm going to have to take a bath any-way...," she said, and crawled to join him.

When she had sat down, she looked straight ahead, and he knew she had come to say something. "You remember," she finally said, "when we was in Mississippi and a rain hit the plantation so the ground was too wet to chop cotton? But it missed a bush bean farm a couple miles away? When we heard the bean farmer was paying cash money, we decided to go pick beans and get rich."

He waited; she didn't expect an answer.

"It must have been a hundred degrees in the shade," she said, "and there we was crawling along those bean rows."

"You and me were behind the others."

Roseanne nodded. "And I collapsed. You never said a word. You just got hold of me under my arms and started dragging me across the bean rows to a shade tree. The bean farmer started yelling, 'He's ruining my beans! He's ruining my beans!'"

"Papa looked back and saw us, and said, 'To hell with your beans!' and came running. So did Mama and Dwight."

Roseanne turned her head and looked at him, waiting.

"Papa collected what pay he could, and we piled in the truck and went back to the plantation."

"Yes. We didn't have much to show for our work, and we didn't have much to eat that night, but we laughed and laughed. It was us—family—against the world." She paused, then said, "But there's times when a body has to step away from family and stand up for self the way you did in yonder."

Talmadge dropped his forehead back onto his arms.

"Don't grieve about it," Roseanne said, then crawled out from under the porch. She stood and brushed the dirt off her dress, then bent over to look at him. "I'm going to pump a tub full of water, let it warm in the sun, then climb in and soak. You'd best do the same before supper."

Mama said nothing to him the rest of that afternoon. She didn't look at him at all. It took all of his will not to try again to make her understand. Anything would be better than this awful silence between them.

After supper, he went to the place on the ditch bank, stretched out on his stomach, and sobbed. It hurt that he had defied her for the first time in his life. It hurt that she had yelled at him with something akin to hate in her face.

Chapter 14

ollowing Roseanne's advice, Talmadge said nothing more to Mama about school, not even when cotton picking began and he sometimes found himself working alongside her. She didn't mention it either, nor did Papa.

On the Saturday afternoon before school started on Monday, he knew he couldn't wait any longer. He went into the kitchen, where Mama and Papa were sitting at the table. Mama was looking at the mail-order catalog, and Papa was reading the *Willowboro News*, which they now subscribed to. Talmadge moistened his lips and said, "Papa, I sure need a haircut before I go back to school."

"I'll do it soon's I read the paper," Papa said. "Won't take long; there ain't that much in it." He looked at Talmadge then, and said, "You need a new shirt and overalls, too. And shoes. After I give you the haircut, why don't you go up to the store and get yourself outfitted." He went back to reading the newspaper.

Mama hadn't looked up at all, but her mouth had thinned and Talmadge had a notion that Papa had put his foot down about school. It wasn't that Mama and Papa didn't argue in front of them sometimes. They did. But when their disagreement involved one of the children, they kept it private. It would have spared him a lot of worry if Papa had told him. He cleared his throat. "I'd like mighty well to have a pair of khaki trousers instead of overalls."

Papa only nodded.

Mama glared at Talmadge and said, "In case you're going to ask next for low-cut shoes, the answer is no."

Papa kept looking at the newspaper.

"Yes, ma'am." He turned and went outside to wait until Papa was ready to cut his hair. Papa was obviously in favor of his continuing to go to school, and Mama had bowed to Papa's wishes. But Mama didn't give up easily; she would probably try again.

After he left the store, where he had seen several

people he knew and watched some checkers games, he stopped at the post office. Miss Hettie handed him a letter from Cousin Maybelle. The return address puzzled him. What were she and Mr. Parks doing in Memphis? Memphis was only about sixty-five miles from Limon, but it was a long way from Rim County. Maybe they were visiting somebody Mr. Parks knew. He had traveled a lot before he went to Rim County and met and married Cousin Maybelle. They were probably coming here next.

When he reached home, he went around to the back, laid the parcel containing his new school outfit on the porch, and went to the pump for a drink of water. He came back and sat on the steps to remove his shoes.

The screen door opened and Missy came out. She sat down by him and gazed glumly toward the barn.

"What's wrong?"

"Betty Ann's mad at me. She don't like me no more."

Missy and Betty Ann's quarrels were nothing to be concerned about. He patted her shoulder.

Missy flinched.

"You mad at me because Betty Ann's mad at you?"

"No, it's that touching makes my skin nervous."

"Okay, I won't pat you. Where is everybody?"

"Mama's mopping the linoleum. Roseanne's curling her hair for church tomorrow."

Peadod—and others—hinted even more strongly nowadays that something was going on between

Roseanne and Mr. Williams. So people liked to gossip. Mr. Williams hadn't even called on Roseanne.

"Where's Dwight?"

"He's laying down."

Getting rested up to go to Riverton tonight, Talmadge thought. Dwight went to Riverton every Saturday night these days. He didn't think Mama knew, but Dwight was spending the cash money he had left on pool games. He was drinking beer, too, and once he had bragged to Talmadge about two girls fussing at each other over him.

Missy sniffled and coughed. "Betty Ann said I always have to have everything my way."

"Is Papa here?"

She shook her head. "He's helping Mr. Teasley add on to his barn."

He rose, picked up the parcel, and went to the screen door. "Is the floor dry? Can I come in?"

"Yes," Mama said. "But don't track in any dirt."

"I just took my shoes off," he said as he went inside. He put the clothes and new shoes on a chair, took the letter from his pocket, and held it up for her to see. She nodded, then picked up the bucket of dirty water to take it outside.

"It's from Cousin Maybelle, and it was postmarked in Memphis."

"Memphis?!" Mama set the bucket down, took the envelope, and studied it. "Well, I declare. What're they doing in Memphis?" She propped the letter against the lamp.

There was no point in trying to get her to open it. She would do as she always did—wait for Papa to open it and read it aloud to all of them.

Papa came home about an hour later, and as usual, he came around to the back instead of going in the front door. Talmadge, sitting on the back porch and leaning against the wall, rose and followed him into the kitchen. Mama stood at one end of the table sifting flour for biscuits. Dwight was up now, sitting at the other end of the table reading the paper. Roseanne was ironing, and Missy was playing jacks. Trying to play jacks. She spent most of her time chasing the rolling ball she had missed on the bounce.

As Papa set his tool chest in its corner, Missy said, "We been waiting for you. We got a letter from Cousin Maybelle." She picked up the jacks and ball and put them into their cloth sack.

"Good," Papa said. He washed and dried his hands, then picked up the letter. "Wonder what they're doing in Memphis," he said.

Roseanne set the flatiron to the back of the stove. Mama put a towel over the biscuits. Dwight folded the paper. They all followed Papa into the front room, and when they were settled, he began to read.

The beginning paragraphs contained the general stuff about how was everybody and they were fine and how various relatives were doing when Cousin Maybelle last saw them. Finally she got down to the explanation they were waiting for.

Me and Frank have moved to Memphis. Frank got more and more discontent in Sweet Spring. He finally decided to turn the store over to Jeremy and we rented out our house.

Missy tilted her head and made a question with her face. Mama motioned for Papa to pause, then said to Missy, "Jeremy is Cousin Maybelle's growed son by her first husband." She nodded to Papa. "Go on, Warren." Papa had his finger at the place he had stopped.

Frank has bought himself a "citified" hardware store and is as happy as a pig in the sunshine.
Speaking for myself, I'm lonesome. Alvira, don't you get lonesome there, so far from kin and friend? Warren, you're good at carpentry. There's building going on here now that times are better. Frank says it's something you might want to consider since machines are about to replace small farmers.

Talmadge scarcely heard the rest—that they would come to visit when they got a new car, that the old one had seen its best days. He felt stunned, and nervous.

Missy rose and kissed Papa on the cheek. "I don't

mind you want us to move, Papa," she said.

Talmadge knew why she said it. There was an eager-
ness in Papa's face, as if he were excited about the
prospect of going to Memphis and doing carpentry
work. For Talmadge, though, starting to school there
would be as hard as it had been in Mississippi and on
Limon. It would be worse. He wouldn't just be a "hillbilly" whose speech sounded strange to flatlanders.
He would be considered a hick. A country hick.

"Wouldn't it be nice to set and embroider with
Maybelle again?" Mama said.

Dwight jumped up. "Papa, it'll be great! We can do
real good in Memphis."

"We got a place here," Papa said, but it was if he were
arguing with himself.

"For right now we have. And I know we can't leave
until the crop's in." Dwight paced, using his hands for
emphasis as he talked. "Don't you see, Papa? With
tractors coming in, Mr. Limon will go to centralized
farming. According to the newspaper, cotton-picking
machines are coming, too. People like us are going to
be out."

"You sure know a lot," Papa said, and although his
voice was mild, Talmadge heard resentment in it. Papa
and Dwight had not been getting along well lately.

Dwight went over to the bed, touched the letter in
Papa's hand, "Listen to what Cousin Maybelle's saying.
There's opportunity in Memphis. There's a future."

Papa looked at the letter again, the yearning so obvious that it might as well be written on his face: All my life I've wanted to be a carpenter.

Talmadge stood up. He couldn't breathe, he had to get out of here. He started to turn around to go through the kitchen and outside, then stopped. Papa's expression had changed. There was doubt in his face. Not doubt. Something else. Something like fear.

Papa looked at him, abruptly laid the letter aside, and said to Talmadge, "We ain't going. It would be nice, though, was you to sometimes consider wants besides your own."

Talmadge lay in bed with his arm across his eyes. Although the track was a half-mile away, the sounds of a freight switching rumbled through the stillness. Next he heard the night passenger train barreling up the track. That meant it was getting on toward midnight. Dwight had not gotten home until a short while ago, long after even Mama and Papa had gone to bed. Talmadge had pretended to be asleep while Dwight stood beside his bed glaring down at him. Dwight was asleep now, snoring. The room smelled of stale beer.

Talmadge turned over, faced the wall. He wished he could go to sleep, wished he didn't know Papa couldn't sleep either. After Dwight came in, the lamp had been lit in the kitchen. Its dim light seeped under and over the door. He heard Papa put a stick of stove wood into the firebox. A little later, the smell of coffee seeped into his room. He didn't have to see; he knew. Papa was sitting at the table reading Cousin Maybelle's letter again.

Chapter 15

The first day back at school had been a good one. Missy was already at the top of the railroad bed, but Talmadge continued to stand near the highway waving back at friends waving at him from inside the bus.

"You better not lallygag," Missy called.

"You and Betty Ann go on," he said. "I'll catch up." He smiled as she lifted eyebrows so pale they seemed almost white against her flushed face. It had been miserably hot on the bus. "Don't worry," he said. "I don't aim to get in trouble." Mama had told them that as soon as they got home, had a bite to eat, and changed their clothes, they were to come to the field.

He stopped again at the top of the railroad mound, stood between the main track and the switch track, and threw out his arms for pure joy. When he boarded the bus this morning, a dozen voices had called out greetings. All day long, he had been treated as if he were somebody special.

The Teasley children disappeared into the two-story house just past the bottom of the incline. Missy and Betty Ann were now even with the Teasleys' sweet potato patch. He walked down the slope.

Betty Ann had gotten ahead of Missy and stopped to wait for her. Missy seemed to be dragging. She still had a cold, but it wasn't a bad one. It was probably weariness from being in a classroom all day. That would be hard on her for a while.

He took out his harmonica and played a snatch of "Fox and Hounds." That was what he was going to play in this year's talent contest. Last year he had been scared to try. He passed the Clarks' house; he was almost to the ditch. Betty Ann had left Missy behind. As she turned into the yard, Missy stumbled. He walked faster.

She was almost to the porch steps. She had changed her mind about going into the house and was heading for the weeds at the side of the yard. Missy was throwing up!

He ran. When he reached her, she leaned weakly against him. "My stomach's been sick most all day," she said. "I didn't eat much of my lunch."

Inside, he helped her wash her face and get undressed down to her petticoat. He put his palm on her forehead the way Mama did. It was something more than first-day jitters. She felt warm, as if she had a little fever. "You got a headache?"

"No. My neck's kind of stiff, but I don't have a headache. You better change and go on to the field."

The fever and runny nose, even being sick at her stomach, were ordinary enough, but the stiff neck was not.

"Does your neck hurt?"

"Kind of."

"Maybe you slept wrong last night and got a crick."

"It's probably from that teacher making me color when I had a headache." She closed her eyes. "Go on, Talmadge. I got to sleep."

"You want me to bring you a glass of water?"

"No! Just go on!"

He had worried for nothing. In real misery, like when she had an earache, Missy was pathetic, not ornery. He went to his room to change out of his school clothes. Dwight's side of the room looked nice. His bed was made; his westerns that were his favorite reading were neatly stacked beneath it alongside a cardboard suitcase and a box containing his winter clothes.

Sitting on his own bed, Talmadge removed his new shoes and sighed with pleasure. Papa had done a good job with building up the heel on the right one, but new shoes made your feet burn.

He rubbed his feet, put on his old shoes and work clothes, then remade his bed, trying to make square tucking corners the way Dwight did. It still didn't look as neat as Dwight's bed. "To heck with it," he said. What he'd like to do was the same as Missy—climb into the bed. But he wasn't sick; he didn't have an excuse. He put on his sun hat.

As he went through the kitchen, he picked up a cold biscuit from a plate covered with a cloth to keep off the flies, made a pocket in it with a table knife, and poured in all the syrup the biscuit could soak up.

On the back porch, he picked up his folded sack, laid it across his shoulder, and started to the field. Jasper came out from under the house and followed him. "Hi, boy," he said. "Ah, I see. You got the notion I'll give you some of my biscuit. Well, syrup's not good for you." He finished it in one bite to keep from tormenting Jasper.

Roseanne's cat came from the barn. "You lonesome, Annabelle?" he asked. "Roseanne'll be home directly." Peadod said Roseanne and Mr. Williams had gotten into a heated argument on the road in front of the church last Wednesday evening after the prayer meeting. Finally, Peadod said, Mr. Williams had turned on his heel and strode away.

Annabelle and Jasper walked with him to the edge of the yard, but there they stopped. Annabelle went back toward the barn; Jasper wagged his tail. "I wish I could stay," Talmadge said. "You can come with me, you know." He laughed when Jasper went the other way, back toward his cool hollow beneath the house.

Squinting at the lowering sun, he stepped into the cornfield. You had to make the stifling walk through the corn to reach the cotton field. Mama was likely stewing by now, but when he told her he had tarried because Missy didn't feel well, she wouldn't be mad at him.

When he reached the end of the cornfield, he saw his family. They were staggered along the rows, all picking this way. Mama's and Papa's glances went beyond him, as if they wondered why Missy wasn't with him. Roseanne, apparently deep in thought, didn't look up. Dwight shot a hard look at him.

Talmadge walked across the two-foot-wide dry and cracked drainage ditch, and up the middle between Mama's rows.

"Yes?" Mama said without pausing in her picking or looking up at him. "Missy's feeling poorly," he told her. "She vomited when we got home from school, and her forehead is warm. I think she's got fever." Mama kept picking; he walked beside one of her rows.

"Less you're experienced," she said, "it's hard to tell when a body's got fever. You got sick ever day the first week you was in school. Sitting in a hot, stuffy room all day is too hard on a young'un."

"And she says her neck is stiff."

Mama faltered, lost her rhythm.

He remembered now. He knew why he had been vaguely worried about the stiff neck. Peadod had told him that Mrs. Williams had complained of a stiff neck before she died of spinal meningitis. "She thinks from having to color when she had a headache," he said.

Mama, who wore khaki pants in the field, stood up. Her hands with the long, big-knuckled fingers and ragged nails rested on the fronts of her thighs while she looked toward the house. Then she turned her head and raised her voice so it would carry to Papa. "Warren— Missy's ailing. I'm going in to check on her."

Papa nodded, but showed no sign of concern. Ailments came and went.

Hefting her half-filled sack to her shoulder, Mama said, "I'll drop it at the end of the field and take new rows when I come back. You can pick these on out."

Talmadge put on his seven-foot sack (the others pulled nine-footers) and bent to the work. He had to pick hard to stay ahead of Dwight, who had begun to hum "School Days."

He knew Dwight blamed him that they were not going to Memphis. But Dwight had turned against him in Mississippi. When Dwight had decided not to go back to school after they left Wild Hog Holler, he had at first been pleased with himself for helping to support the family. His self-pride had been gone a long time, though. He now clearly hated farming, hated being

Papa's helper, and, Talmadge felt sure, resented that Talmadge got out of a lot of field work because he did go to school.

The humming grew closer; Dwight was gaining on him. Dwight stopped humming and began to supply words. "School boy, school boy, precious little school boy...."

Talmadge took deep breaths and blew them out. He tried to turn his mind to something else—to LaVerne, to Assembly, to his new teacher, Miss Brady. It didn't work. The anger was in him the same way it had been the day Stinky took his book and dropped it on the ground.

Chapter 16

He finished a little ahead of Dwight, stood waiting until Dwight straightened up. "I know why you do things like that. You're jealous of me going to school!"

"Jealous of you?! Jealous of Papa's little pet?"

"So jealous your liver's turned to bile!"

Dwight flipped his sack strap over his head and with the ends of his fingers poked Talmadge just below his ribs. "How about your liver? It okay?" Dwight poked again, this time on his stomach. "Or maybe it's your belly."

Talmadge threw off his sack strap and swung, aiming for the spot high on the jaw.

Dwight dodged; the blow only grazed the side of his head. He made a grab for Talmadge.

He managed to step out of reach. In a fistfight he had a chance. In a wrestling match, Dwight would pin him and he'd have to give. But he couldn't move fast enough to escape Dwight's next grab for him. Dwight had a grip on his left shoulder; he was about to get thrown. Then Dwight made a mistake, didn't move in close quickly enough. Talmadge put a hard, short right jab into his ribs.

Dwight turned him loose and doubled his fists. "Okay, you want it that way," he said, and now they were circling, watching for an opening.

Talmadge was dimly aware that Papa was coming. But it didn't sink into his consciousness. There were two people in the world right now, and one was him and the other Dwight. He didn't realize what was about to happen until Papa slammed a cotton stalk, unopened bolls and all, across Dwight's back. The blow was so hard some of the green bolls popped off.

Dwight arched his shoulders and gasped.

The stalk came again. His face contorted, ugly, Papa yelled, "Can't you never leave people alone?"

Talmadge's words burst out, like a scream. "Papa—no!"

The cotton stalk, raised to strike Dwight again, came at him instead. He flinched under the blow, braced himself for the next one. It didn't come. Papa dropped the tattered stalk and strode away.

"Bastard," Dwight said under his breath.

"Yeah."

"Because he gave you a lick, too? One lick to show how fair he is?!" Dwight swiped his arm across his eyes, grabbed his sack, flung it over between his next two rows, put the strap across his shoulder, and started picking. "Hell, you're his little hero! It was me quit school to help him. But it's because of you he won't even think about moving to Memphis!"

"That ain't true!"

On his knees and snatching cotton from the burrs, his face hard, Dwight looked back at him.

"I mean," Talmadge said, "when Papa was sitting there gazing at the letter from Cousin Maybelle after he read it aloud, there was something...." His voice trailed off. How could he explain? He had seen fear on Papa's face. But fear of what? Maybe Papa had been thinking about what Dwight said, that there was no future for them here. But Talmadge didn't think that was it. Something else had scared Papa, something in that letter.

Chapter 17

Talmadge was relieved to find Missy out of bed and sitting on the back steps when they went home at the end of the day.

"Mama gave me some of that medicine she makes," Missy said. "The coltsfoot syrup. It made me feel better."

"I'm glad." He put his hand on her shoulder, and she flinched.

"I forgot. Touching makes your skin nervous." He crossed the porch and went inside.

At the supper table, he and Dwight and Papa and Roseanne ate without talking, their eyes on their plates. There was a hurt in Dwight's face, a tightness around his mouth, that scared Talmadge. Ordinarily Mama would demand to know what was wrong, but because of her concern about Missy, who hadn't wanted any supper, she didn't seem to notice.

Dwight went to bed at dusk. Talmadge soon followed him. He was so exhausted, he felt himself sinking into sleep minutes after he lay down.

He awakened suddenly. Moonlight streamed through the east windows. Something, he thought groggily, was missing in here. He shook his head to clear away the sleep fuzz and sat up. Dwight was not in his bed. Why had that brought him out of sleep? Dwight had probably just gone outside to the toilet. He started to lie back down, but straightened up again. Dwight's bed was made. Not made as neatly as usual, but the top sheet was pulled up.

Something else was different. Something was missing. The suitcase beneath Dwight's bed! The suitcase was gone!

Dwight had run away? He was hitchhiking at night? He would have waited until near daybreak, wouldn't he? The track—a freight. If a freight didn't switch for the night passenger train, another would for a northbound freight. Dwight would just sit and wait.

Talmadge yanked on his overalls and shirt, grabbed his old shoes, slipped out of his room and through the kitchen. He held the screen door to keep it from snapping shut. On the back steps, he put on the shoes.

Dwight had done it just this way; that's why Talmadge hadn't awakened immediately.

Running, walking, running again, he headed for the track. At first he was not aware that he had company. Then he heard the feet touching lightly on the gravel, and Jasper ranged in front of him, trotting and waiting, and trotting again. In the cool of the night, Jasper was like a young dog again.

He was halfway between the Clarks' and the Teasleys' houses when he knew that a freight train was switching. He heard its whistle, the rumble, the slow clacking as the wheels crossed the spaces between rails. He had heard the men at the store talking. They said in really hard times, mostly in '31 and '32, family men had ridden the rails looking for work. But nowadays hoboes were apt to be mean as boar hogs. He ran again; now he was at the bottom of the railroad bed.

The freight train, a fairly long one, was coming to a halt. The moon threw enough light that he could see all the cars to the north of the road, and some of the ones down the track. None of the doors were open.

He skirted the edge of the Teasleys' yard that ran parallel to the shallow ditch at the bottom of the steep track bed, passed their lot, and came to the edge of their cornfield. He still didn't see a boxcar with its door ajar.

The passenger train's whistle, strident and demanding, warned at a crossroad. He had to get on the other side, the shadowed side, of the freight train. Had to cross the shallow ditch, crawl up the bank. Thankfully, the ditch was dry. But it was grown over; there could be snakes. He was cold, but he was sweating. Jasper sat looking up at him. "Let's go," he said in a hoarse whisper, but his body didn't obey. Jasper started, looked back. Talmadge plunged into the cattails, hit the small rocks at the bottom of the incline, scrambled up through vines that grew through the rocks. He was at the top of the bed; his heart pounded in his ears. He could climb over the coupling between two boxcars. No. Between his bad foot and being clumsy, plus the chance that one of the railroad crew might spot him if he stood and walked to the end of the boxcar in front of him, he would do better to go under it.

It was very dark beneath the boxcar; the smells of iron and grease were strong in his nostrils. If the rimmed iron wheels moved, they would cut him into pieces.

Then he was on the other side, the dark side. He stood, walked quickly but carefully across the main track, and went a few feet down the slope. There, a partially opened door, and standing in it, a form. A man. It wasn't Dwight, but that's the car Dwight would be in. The man would have given him a hand up.

The passenger train's bright light was bearing down, the roar was deafening. Talmadge dropped to his knees, hunkered down with his hands over his ears until it was past him. He stood then, and ran toward the boxcar with the partially open door. "Dwight!" he screamed. "Dwight!"

The freight train jerked, began to move, the man figure disappeared into the blackness inside the boxcar.

From below and to the north of where he was, Dwight's voice called: "Talmadge?"

The freight train gathered speed, and he saw Dwight sitting near the bottom of the bank. Slipping and sliding on the rocks, he went to Dwight and dropped down beside him.

They sat in silence. A car, its lights bright in the darkness, approached, and then sped on down the highway. Dwight stood, Talmadge stood. They made their way up to the main track, walked between the rails to their road. They were beyond the Teasleys' sweet potato patch when Talmadge realized that Dwight was shortening his stride beyond comfort to keep in step with him. Jasper trotted ahead of them.

Dwight changed the suitcase from his right to his left hand. "Why did you come after me?"

"I didn't think any why's."

They were silent again. Then Dwight said, "What I said this afternoon—about quitting school to help Papa—it ain't true. It was hard enough to go to school in Wild Hog Holler where everybody knew us." He took a deep breath. "I lied even to myself. The truth is, I didn't go in Mississippi because I couldn't take those strangers seeing how dumb I am."

"You're not dumb."

"I'm not smart in books like you." Dwight gave a short, harsh laugh. "Of course, Mama was proud of me for quitting to 'help Papa.' I got it into my head that he wasn't—that he didn't even appreciate my great sacrifice. That it was you he was really proud of. I've been taking it out on you. Lately, I've been smart-mouthing Papa, too. When he laid into me today.... It wasn't just me tormenting you got him to that point."

Talmadge could picture how it had happened: Dwight making sarcastic remarks to Papa; Papa taking it silently, letting it build, until this afternoon when Dwight had turned the sarcasm against Talmadge and provoked him to fight. Papa hadn't stopped to think; something had snapped inside him and he had gone berserk.

As he and Dwight turned into the yard, Talmadge saw Papa, fully clothed, sitting on the porch, his feet on the top step. When he and Dwight reached the bottom of the steps, he was sure Papa would say something, apologize to Dwight, say he was glad to see them, that he had worried. He didn't. His body appearing thinner and his shoulders more bent than ever in the moonlight, he stood and then went inside.

Chapter 18

According to the clock in Talmadge's head, it was six a.m. Time to get up. Dwight and the others had already left for the field. Last night.... It had really happened. It hadn't been a dream. He heard Mama moving around in the kitchen; she hadn't gone to the field. Missy must still be sick. Talmadge groaned and sat up.

"Morning, Mama," he said when he went into the kitchen.

"Morning."

She didn't sound as if she were upset. He didn't think she knew what had happened in the field yesterday, or that Dwight had almost run away last night.

He went out to the toilet, saw that Mama had already done a washing and hung it on the line. The Golden Buff Minorcas, now full-grown, were clucking and scratching in the yard. When he came back inside after washing his hands and face at the pump, he asked, "Is Missy still sick? Is that why you didn't go to the field this morning?"

She put some oatmeal in a bowl for him. "Roseanne said Missy was restless last night—tossing and turning and mumbling in her sleep. I'm going to keep her home today. She feels all right when she gets up, she can go with me to the field and play on a pallet in the wagon shade."

He nodded and ate his oatmeal while she swept the back porch. When he went into his room to get ready for school, he heard her come back into the kitchen. Now she was washing his bowl and spoon and the oatmeal pan.

"I'll make your lunch today," she said when he came out of his room.

He had made his and Missy's lunches yesterday morning. "While you're doing it," he said, "I'll pump a trough of water."

When he came back inside, she still didn't have his lunch ready. The kitchen clock said seven-thirty. If she didn't hurry, he wouldn't get up to the highway in time to catch the bus. He would have to walk the long way to school.

"It wouldn't hurt you to stay out and help today," Mama said. "I've heared some young'uns stay out till the first picking's over."

His temper began to rise. "You can make up lessons," he said, "but you can't ever make up other things you...."

A choked cry of terror cut short his reply.

Talmadge's mouth was still open but his next word dissolved. Mama's hands, one on the jelly jar, the other twisting the lid, froze.

"Talmadge!" Missy screamed again.

His neck hair rose; he ran. Mama overtook him within three steps.

Missy, her thin chest heaving, was lying flat on her back with her arms thrown out. "I didn't know you was here, Mama," she said. "I went to get up, but my leg—something's wrong with one of my legs."

Mama whipped the sheet off of Missy's legs. "The muscles is spasming," she said, and began massaging Missy's right leg.

"Don't!" Missy screeched. "It hurts. My head hurts. I hurt everywhere."

Mama straightened and gazed down at her. "Ride that mule Goliath up to the store, Talmadge, and ask Mr. Limon—or whoever's there—to call the doctor."

"Dr. Spain," he said. Dr. Spain would know what to do.

Chapter 19

Mama opened the front door for Dr. Spain. Since Talmadge had only seen him in his car, he hadn't realized that Dr. Spain was a good six feet tall. Like Mama, he had big bones, and his hands were large and thick-fingered. He had a slight limp, which Talmadge doubted most people even noticed.

The doctor removed his hat, and at the same time he was returning Mama's greetings, walked over and put it on the chifforobe. The top of his large head was bald, but he didn't look as old as Papa.

He immediately went into Missy's room, spoke to her in a cheerful, booming voice, and sat down in the straight chair Mama had placed beside the bed. Mama went in with him. Talmadge stayed in the front room, standing at the foot of Mama and Papa's bed. He could see everything that was going on, but he wasn't in the way.

Dr. Spain took Missy's temperature, listened to her chest with a stethoscope, asked her questions, and joked with her. Talmadge could see her relaxing a little. "Now, little lady," Dr. Spain said, "I want you to touch your chin to your chest."

"I can't. My neck's stiff."

"Try."

She tried and started crying.

Mama took a step toward her, and stopped. Mama had put on her Sunday dress for Dr. Spain's visit, and her good shoes.

Cradling the back of Missy's head and neck with one of his big hands, Dr. Spain said, "I'm sorry, hon. It's an important test." He gazed at Missy a minute, then looked through the door. "You did a good job of describing her symptoms, Talmadge."

"Thank you." The telephone was upstairs in Mr. Limon's office. Mr. Limon hadn't been there. Mr. Baldridge, the storekeeper, had told Talmadge to come upstairs with him to telephone Dr. Spain. He had been nervous about talking on a telephone, but the nervousness had passed as he concentrated on answering Dr. Spain's questions. He had only been back home a few minutes when Dr. Spain arrived.

The doctor rubbed his hand over his head as if he

had forgotten he didn't have hair to smooth down.

What is it, Dr. Spain? Talmadge wanted to ask. Even if it was spinal meningitis, they had to know.

Finally, Dr. Spain said, "What we have here is infantile paralysis."

Talmadge took hold of the bedpost.

Mama didn't move; her expression didn't change. He didn't think she understood the seriousness of infantile paralysis. He did. They had talked about it in health class last year. Talked about President Roosevelt's having been struck with it when he was a grown man, so the word infantile was wrong. But mostly children got it, and sometimes, they died.

Mama's mouth worked. "My boy Dwight," she got out, "read to me from the newspaper that it were around."

She did know about infantile paralysis!

Dr. Spain nodded. "It's supposed to be a disease you watch for in June, but this time it struck in late August. This is the seventh case in the county."

"Am—am I going to die?"

"No, little lady," Dr. Spain said, "you're not going to die."

Talmadge's relief went as swiftly as it had come. President Roosevelt had to wear heavy braces and could hardly walk; mostly he got around in a wheelchair.

"I'm inclined to think you're lucky," Dr. Spain told Missy.

Lucky. Missy's case was evidently not nearly as serious as President Roosevelt's had been.

Mama wet her lips. "I don't hold much with hospitals," she said. "But iffen you think...."

"I agree with you when it comes to Willowboro Hospital," Dr. Spain said.

That Dr. Spain didn't like Willowboro Hospital was common knowledge. John Edward said that if one of his patients had to go to a hospital, Dr. Spain sent them all the way to Memphis. Missy had never spent a single night away from home. And Missy was Mama's heart. Mama couldn't stand it if Missy had to go away to a hospital. None of them could. Missy couldn't either. She looked scared.

"For the time being, we're going to take care of her right here at home," Dr. Spain said.

For the time being. Did that mean he could treat Missy at home unless complications arose?

"Now, Missy," Dr. Spain said, "I'm going to take some measurements of your leg so I can get a splint for it. Until I bring it—hopefully tomorrow—I'm going to make your leg behave with some small sandbags." He looked at Talmadge. "The sandbags are in the back seat of my car."

"Yes, sir," Talmadge said. Feeling important, he went out to Dr. Spain's car and got the sandbags. As he went back into the front room, he heard Dr. Spain saying to Missy in a low, calm voice, "The shot I just gave you was to keep down the pain, but it's still going to hurt some when I straighten your leg."

Missy cried out when Dr. Spain pulled her leg into its proper position, and Talmadge worried that Mama might rush over and try to comfort her. But she didn't. Her face expressionless, she stood like a stump. She was sweating something awful; the dress material was three shades darker around her armpits.

Dr. Spain talked in a soothing voice, and Missy's eyelids drooped. "Go to sleep now, sweetheart," Dr. Spain said.

As he came out of Missy's room, he said, "Come along while I wash my hands."

Walking behind Mama and the doctor to the kitchen, Talmadge studied Dr. Spain's feet and shoes and knew what caused the limp. Dr. Spain had a clubfoot!

Washing his hands as Talmadge had never seen anybody wash their hands—soaping and soaping them, then rinsing and drying, even between his fingers—Dr. Spain asked, "What grade are you in, son?"

"I'm in the seventh." It made him proud to say it.

"Anybody else in school?"

In a wooden-sounding voice, Mama said, "No, sir. Roseanne never did take to it. And Dwight quit to help his daddy."

"They're in the field?"

"Them and my husband. Yes, they're in the field."

Dr. Spain nodded. "You saw me wash my hands just

now. It's imperative that all of you wash your hands after you tend Missy."

Talmadge bit his lower lip. He had tended Missy yesterday when she threw up. And he hadn't washed his hands before he ate the biscuit filled with syrup. But he had wet the washrag to sponge Missy's face. Surely that would count.

Dr. Spain gave Mama some pain pills for Missy, then said, "None of you can have any contact with anybody outside the family for two weeks."

Two weeks! He would have to miss two whole weeks of school.

"We don't have a cotton house for storage," Mama said.

"As long as he doesn't go inside the gin or into the store, there's no reason Mr. McLinn can't take in the cotton," Dr. Spain said.

That was right. You didn't need to have contact with anybody when you went to the gin. The wagon just pulled in under an overhang and a big pipe sucked up the cotton.

"For that matter," Dr. Spain said, "we don't really know how infantile paralysis spreads. Cases are often isolated, and most of the time, only one in a family is stricken. But the rule is no outside contact for fourteen days. I'm going to have to tack up a quarantine sign."

Mama nodded.

Dr. Spain left the kitchen, talking as he went. "When

I leave here I'll go by the school." He picked up his hat from the top of the chifforobe. Talmadge held the screen door open for him and walked with him across the porch and down the steps.

"About your clubfoot, Talmadge, I know a good orthopedic surgeon in Memphis. As young as you are, it's possible.... But first things first. Right now we'll take care of Missy."

We'll take care of Missy. The doctor was treating him like an assistant. As for his foot, he didn't want to get his hopes up. Dr. Spain had only said, "it's possible."

Dr. Spain opened the car door, put his satchel in the car, and reached under the seat. He took out a tack hammer and a yellow and black cardboard sign, and went back toward the porch. Talmadge walked beside him. "Her leg, it.... It's going to get well ain't—isn't—it?"

Dr. Spain brought the hand holding the hammer up and lightly rubbed the side of his nose with his thumb as he answered with a cheerful voice. "If we keep it straight.... That's the thing to do now. Keep it straight."

Talmadge drew in his breath. Mama had taught him to understand body talk when he was a child. Not only Mama, but other people, watched movements more intently than they listened to words. And he knew for a fact that you could rely on body language more than you could on words. Dr. Spain didn't think Missy's leg would ever get well.

Chapter 20

When Talmadge went back inside, Mama stood in the front room gazing at Missy's closed door. The circles under her armpits were beginning to dry. The sickly sweet smell of her talcum powder mixed with the odor of her sweat. She settled into the rocker, untied and loosened the laces of her Sunday shoes.

Sitting down on the floor to remove his school shoes, he pictured Dr. Spain rubbing the side of his nose with his thumb, which meant "lie," as he answered Talmadge's question as to whether Missy would be crippled. Dr. Spain hadn't actually said Missy would not be crippled. But his body had taken his dodging the question as a lie. His tone had been cheerful, though, as if he had reason to hope, even if he didn't really believe.

Mama put her shoes in their box, folded the tissue over them, put the top on the box, went to the bed and put the box beneath it, then sat down in the rocker again. Gazing at Missy's closed door, she said in a low, sad voice, "What good's a straight leg if she can't walk on it? The doctor gives the notion she's going to get well, but what he's thinking is that she'll be a cripple."

Mama had not even seen what he had. But she was better at reading body language than he. Talmadge picked up his shoes and stood. "He....I expect it's that he's doubtful about being hopeful."

Puzzlement crossed Mama's face, then she said, "I ain't going against him if that's why you're saying whatever it is you're saying." She looked toward Missy's door again and he thought she was going to cry. He hadn't seen Mama cry since he was little and she wept about the hard feelings between her and Papa's families. He wanted to hug her, comfort her. But it was as if an invisible wall stood between them. He moistened his lips. "I'll put on my work clothes and go on to the field."

Mama stood, too, and when she spoke again, her voice was firm. "I'd as soon you don't go to the field till after dinner. After you change your clothes, you might get the kaiser blade and cut down the weeds along the path to the toilet. When you're through with that, it wouldn't hurt if you gave your room a good sweeping."

"Yes, ma'am." She was right; it was her place to tell the others.

When they came home at noon, she waited until they had washed their hands and faces. But before they sat down to eat, she said, "The doctor's been here. He says Missy's got infantile paralysis in her right leg. He didn't say it, but he thinks she'll be a cripple the rest of her life."

For a minute, there was shocked silence, then Dwight's face started working and he stumbled outside. Talmadge could hear him sobbing, a harsh, tearing sound, as if the sobs were breaking loose from chains. Mama ought to have prepared them, been gentler with her telling.

Roseanne didn't make a sound, but tears slid down her cheeks. She wiped them away with her fingertips and left the kitchen. Talmadge knew she was going to her and Missy's room.

Papa stood completely still. He straightened his spine until Talmadge feared it would snap. His eyes—Papa's blue eyes that generally held a faraway sadness—turned hard as glass. A freight whistled in the distance; the sparrows' twittering floated through the open door. But there was no sound in the kitchen.

Mama broke the silence. "Warren?" she said in a frightened voice. "Warren, are you all right?"

Papa didn't answer. He stood like a wooden statue clothed with blue overalls and blue work shirt and grayed undershirt showing where the top two shirt buttons were opened.

Roseanne came back into the kitchen.

Slowly Papa turned his head and looked at her. "You prayed, daughter?"

"Yes, Papa."

"And for what did you pray?"

"Why, for His healing touch. For His mercy."

"There ain't nothing merciful about Him!"

Roseanne gasped and took a step backward.

"Warren—don't." Mama tried to put her arms around Papa. He pushed her away.

What Papa had said scared Talmadge, too. He half expected God to drop Papa dead on the spot. None of them spoke as he went back outside, crossed the yard, and stepped into the cornfield.

At the first afternoon weigh-up, Talmadge's sack was so full, Papa had trouble bending it to hang it on the scale. He moved the weight to a higher and higher figure. The bar balanced. Forty-six pounds. Roseanne's eyebrows went up. Dwight whistled. He had beaten Dwight by three pounds. And it meant nothing.

The weighing and emptying done, Talmadge took

another swallow of the tepid water from the jar under the wagon. Fresh and cold from the pump, the water was delicious. Warm, it tasted like old iron.

Papa picked up his empty sack. Talmadge picked up his.

"Papa, Talmadge, stay and rest," Roseanne said.

"I'm all right," Talmadge said.

Papa didn't say anything.

At his rows Talmadge bent over and started working again. If you did it right, picking cotton was an exacting job. You needed rhythm and a pattern that kept the cotton flowing from burrs to both hands to one hand to sack, and at the same time you had to avoid getting flakes of crisp, papery brown leaves and hull fringe in with the cotton.

His hands moved up and down the tall stalks growing in the rich black soil, moved rapidly from one stalk to the next when he crossed sand blows where the stalks were drought-burned and stunted. He walked on his knees when his back gave out, then bent from the waist again when his knees gave out.

Before the final weigh-up, he was spent. His right leg ached; his back hurt. His hands trembled, and he wondered if he had strength left for the walk home. Somewhere in the back of his mind, he had thought he could replace Mama in the field. He couldn't.

He was too tired to eat much supper. Dwight told him to rest, that he would pump a trough of water and slop the pigs. Talmadge took the wash pan out on the back porch and soaked his feet. That done, he sat with his legs dangling off the porch and stroked Jasper. "Pretty soon it'll be cool," he said. "Winter'll come and maybe it'll snow. You and me can track rabbits." He pulled Jasper onto his lap and hugged him so close Jasper wiggled to be let loose.

He sat there for a long time. The evening star began to glow; another star came out. The sky deepened to a purplish blue. In his mind's eye, he saw Missy when she learned to skip, saw her running to throw her arms around his waist when he came home from school.

The Clarks were singing on their front porch. The voices blended in sweet, sad harmony. Talmadge took out his harmonica and played along as they sang, "Down in the valley, valley so low—late in the evening, hear the wind blow." He played through the chorus, but in the middle of the next verse, "Roses love sunshine, violets love dew; angels in heaven know I love you," his throat closed, and the tears began to flow.

Chapter 21

Mama was making hotcakes when Talmadge finished his morning chores and went inside. It seemed as if Missy had been sick for a long time, but this was only Thursday, the third day. Yesterday, Dr. Spain had splinted her leg.

It would be a few minutes before the hotcakes were ready; he needed to see Missy. He went to her doorway. Her yellow hair was fanned out on the pillow and her eyes were closed. Dried tears made a trail from the corners of her eyes down the sides of her face. He gave a shuddering sigh and turned to go back to the kitchen.

"Talmadge."

She didn't open her eyes when he went in and took her hand, which was hot and dry.

"Did I wake you up last night when I cried?" Her voice came slow and tired.

"I was so wore out I slept like a log."

"I woke Roseanne up. She sat beside my bed and sung me a lullaby."

"Can't anybody sing lullabies prettier than Roseanne."

"One time Papa took me in the front room and rocked me. But he couldn't cuddle me right because of the splint."

"Papa used to rock me when I had bad dreams."

After a silence, Missy said, "I'm sorry about you missing school."

Sick as she was, she was thinking about him. He had to swallow hard before he said, "Don't worry about me missing school. I'll catch up." Tears were sliding down the sides of her face again as he left for the kitchen.

The others were eating. Three plate-sized hotcakes were stacked on his plate. Butter oozed from the pat in the center of the top one and down the sides of the cakes under it. He started to sit down, remembered that he hadn't washed his hands.

"Don't be sparing with the soap," Mama said. "I can always make more soap."

They ate in silence until Roseanne pushed back her plate. "I don't want the rest," she said. She hadn't touched half of her stack of hotcakes.

The day passed. Night came. Morning. Day. Friday evening. Behind them, more cotton bolls were bursting open. Ahead of them, cotton hung loose in the brown burrs. If it should rain hard, the locks would fall to the ground and be ruined.

On Saturday morning, Roseanne stayed with Missy, and Mama came to the field. She couldn't maintain her rhythm. Sometimes she stopped picking altogether, stood, and looked toward the house.

At dinner, before he went to take another load of cotton to the gin, Papa said, "From now till Monday, don't nobody even think about that cotton field."

Talmadge doubted Papa would be able to stop thinking about it. The first picking was the most crucial. But there would be two more, and when it turned cold, the snapping.

That evening when they went into the front room after supper, Missy called, "Why is everybody so quiet?"

Papa went to her door. "We're trying not to disturb you."

"I'm lonesome," Missy said. "I want to come in there."

Papa brought her in, sat her on his and Mama's bed, and put pillows between her back and the head of the bed.

"Singing might calm my leg down," Missy said. "It's trying to get out of the splint."

"That's why the doctor put on the splint," Roseanne

said in her gentle voice. "To keep your leg muscles in place."

Mama's face became grim, but she didn't say anything, and after a moment, her expression smoothed and she began to hum a tune they all knew. Roseanne with her clear soprano and Mama with her alto began:

> Slack your rope, hangman,
> O slack it for a while;
> I think I see my father coming,
> Riding many a mile.
> O father have you brought me gold?
> Or have you paid my fee?
> Or have you come to see me hanging
> On the gallows tree?

Papa and Dwight and Talmadge sang:

> I have not brought you gold;
> I have not paid your fee;
> But I have come to see you hanging
> On the gallows tree.

Roseanne grasped her throat and lolled her tongue. Missy laughed and clapped. "Now I want Talmadge to play his mouth organ. The one about the fox and hounds."

Smiling at him, his family nodded encouragement.

He took his harmonica from his pocket, ran the scale. "I'm going to play 'Fox and Hounds' in the talent show at school," he said, "so I need the practice."

"Tell the story first," Missy said.

"You're right. I need to practice the story, too. There's four hounds, and there ain't anything hounds would rather do than chase a fox. Here they come." He blew the heavy, menacing notes for the hounds.

"And there goes the little fox, running lickety-split for the woods." He made the quick, airy notes for the fox. "He gets across the meadow and into the woods, but the dogs are gaining on him. Their tongues are hanging out and they're slavering and their eyes are yellow."

"That little fox is afeared, ain't he?" Missy said.

"Sure he is. But he don't give up. He just runs faster, and he's thinking all the time about how he's going to get out of the predicament he's in. You'll hear it when the dogs start snuffling because they think they've got him cornered in a hollow log. But they don't. The fox has left his scent all around the end of that log, then he's scooted right through it and out the other end and is long gone. Now I'm going to play the story."

At the end there was the sound of the fox running, his heart beating like a trip-hammer, and farther and farther behind him, the hounds, until you could only hear the fox when he slowed down and finally stopped running.

After a silence, Missy said, "That was wonderful."

"Yes," Mama said, "it was." She got up to light the lamp.

Talmadge was ready for sleep. For the first time since Missy had become sick, he was relaxed.

Chapter 22

On Monday evening, Talmadge had a slight headache. Mama's bad mood wasn't helping it any. He could understand; between washing Missy's bedclothes, tending her day and night, preparing meals, and doing regular housework, she was so exhausted she had circles under her eyes.

After supper, he told Papa he was really tired and asked if he could be excused from helping with evening chores. There was no point in mentioning the headache and having them worry, too.

Papa nodded. "You been working too hard. Why don't you sit out on the front porch? There's a breeze blowing."

When he walked out onto the porch, he saw Mr. Teasley, a fine-looking man with wide shoulders, pulling a red wagon up the road. Mr. Teasley waved and motioned toward the wagon. He must be bringing something for Missy, Talmadge thought. He went down the steps and walked toward the road, but stopped on the yard side of the wagon drive over the small drainage ditch that ran beside the road.

"How's Missy?" Mr. Teasley asked as he stopped.

"She's not doing too good."

Looking sad, Mr. Teasley nodded. "Upon Dr. Spain's advice, everybody waited a few days to...." He motioned toward the wagon. "We seem to have been made the receiving station, which is our pleasure. Your teacher sent your books and assignments so you wouldn't get behind."

"That was mighty kind of her." He was glad to get his books.

"The cake's from Mrs. Teasley."

"Chocolate cake's our favorite." He looked back at the quarantine sign. "I don't know whether it includes the yard or not."

"I don't either," Mr. Teasley said. "Maybe I'd better give you the cake, and I'll put the other things here beside the road."

"Yes, sir." He took the cake and put it on the porch. Ordinarily he would be tempted to take a finger swipe of the frosting. But right now, just the thought of eating chocolate frosting made him sick to his stomach.

Mr. Teasley waved and left with the wagon.

Talmadge took everything to the porch. There was a paper-doll book for Missy from her teacher and drawings from the other first-graders. In addition to his books, there were folded letters to him. And an envelope with "Roseanne McLinn" written on it. "Matthew Williams" was written in the upper left-hand corner. He turned the envelope over. There were three letters on the seal flap: I.L.U. I love you! Peadod had been right all along.

Since Missy was quiet right now, maybe sleeping, he decided to leave the cutout book and drawings on the porch for the moment. He would also get his letters and books later. He put the letter to Roseanne between his overall bib and his shirt, picked up the cake, took it to the screen door, set it down again while he opened the door. Holding the door open with his right foot, he again picked up the cake, and took it to the kitchen.

Roseanne was drying what appeared to be the last plate; Mama was scrubbing a pot, her back to him, when he set the cake on the table and said, "Mrs. Teasley sent a chocolate cake."

Mama glanced over her shoulder and said, "That was mighty nice of her." She went back to scrubbing the pot.

To Roseanne he mouthed, "Mr. Williams," slid out

the edge of the envelope from behind his overall bib,
then pushed it back. Aloud he said, "Miss Brady sent
my books and my notebook and homework assignments. There's a paper-doll book and drawings for
Missy."

"Oh, I want to see them," Roseanne said.

When they had gone through the front room and onto
the porch, he gave her the letter.

She opened the envelope, unfolded a single sheet
of tablet paper, and moved her lips while she read what
Talmadge figured must surely be the shortest letter ever
written. As far as he could tell, there were only four
words.

When Roseanne went back inside, he opened his
own letters. LaVerne's said:

Dear Talmadge,
Our new teacher is strict! I don't mind too much,
though. You sure got good-looking over the summer.
We're all praying for Missy.
Your friend,
LaVerne

That was all except for drawings, more like doodles, of
a flower, a heart with an arrow through it, a bird, and
a comic face with one crossed eye and a sad, turned-
down mouth.

She might have written more, Talmadge thought. But

it was nice of her to say he had gotten good-looking over the summer. He refolded her letter and read John Edward's. John Edward had done some research on infantile paralysis. It went back to ancient Egyptian times, he wrote, and, Talmadge might find interesting, it was originally known as the clubfoot disease.

He slapped at a mosquito that had settled on his face, and the slap jarred his head. The headache seemed to be worse; in fact he felt achy all over. He rubbed the back of his neck and read Meg Weston's long, newsy letter. Last, he unfolded Peadod's. Scrawled in his almost illegible hand, Peadod began, "Hi, Buddy," then said it "tuched" his "hart" when children suffered. Talmadge's eyes stung. He took Peadod for granted, and he sometimes joined the other boys in teasing Peadod. When he went back to school, it would never happen again.

His hand strayed to his neck again. His neck! He bent his head toward his chest. It didn't hurt any worse. It must just be that the headache made his neck tense. He read the rest of the letters, went inside, and took his books in to the kitchen table. He may as well start. He had a lot of catching up to do. Roseanne must be out back. Mama was now wiping the stove. "You about through in here?" he asked. "I want to do my lessons."

"Then do them!" She squinted at him. "You feel all right?"

"I feel fine," he said, louder than he meant to.

"You don't have to holler. My hearing ain't gone yet." She closed her eyes, then said, "Oh, mercy."

She had heard before he did. Missy was calling Mama. She went to Missy's room, came back, dipped a glass of water, and reached up in the cabinet for Missy's pain pills. She shook one of the pills into her palm, and returned the bottle to the shelf.

Good, Talmadge thought as she left. Now he could get something done. He would do his arithmetic first because it was his worst subject. He took out a sheet of paper, and read the first problem:

> *Joan's mother had one-fourth of a pie left from dinner. She gave Joan and two friends each one-third of the leftover pie. What fraction of the whole pie did each girl get?*

Rubbing his forehead, he read it again. He didn't care how much pie each one got! Why did it have to be pie anyway?

He snapped the book shut just as Mama came back into the kitchen. "I thought you was missing school," she said.

"I am. But not because of this crazy arithmetic book. I mostly miss school because of my friends." He bit his lip. He shouldn't have said that. He didn't really mean it, not the way it sounded.

"Yes," Mama said, "that's the way I figure it."

There was no point in trying to explain to her. "Shoot," he said as he jerked the book open again.

She stepped up behind him and grabbed a handful of his hair. "What was that you said?"

"I said shoot!"

"It didn't sound like shoot to me."

"It was. I said shoot. I didn't say that other word you thought I did."

"I know what I heared," she said, but she took her fingers out of his hair.

Papa came in through the back door and picked up a chair. "Come on, Alvira. Let's you and me set out on the front porch."

She didn't respond to Papa. Glaring at Talmadge, she said, "Don't seem to me getting up to seventh grade has made you so all-fired smart. Smart aleck's more like it."

"Alvira."

"I'm coming!"

She was leaving—finally. She made him so mad he could spit. Not spit. He hadn't said the word she despised and she had pulled his hair and as much as called him a liar. Across the top line of the sheet of notebook paper, he wrote the word he hadn't said. It made him feel good to write it. He wrote it again, wrote a whole line.

"Just a minute, I forgot my wedding band."

She was coming back! Talmadge wadded up the

page. He peered at his open book, frowning as if he were trying to understand a problem.

"We ain't so rich you can throw away paper neither!" She snatched up the ball of paper and smoothed it out. "Now you use that there for scratch paper."

Talmadge stared at the paper while she straightened it, kept staring at it while she got her wedding band from the corner of the shelf where she put it when she washed dishes.

She had looked right at the sheet of paper. She had kept looking at it while she smoothed it with her hand. She didn't know what the words said. Mama couldn't read!

He didn't move until the front screen door opened and closed. Then he folded the paper beneath the writing and lifted the oilcloth. With the paper fold-line against the table edge, he tore it off and ripped the strip into tiny pieces.

He should have realized she couldn't read. He had realized it. Somewhere behind a closed door in his mind he had known. She had never helped any of them with homework. She waited for Papa to read letters aloud. She pretended to read the envelopes, but she didn't. She only recognized the handwriting. He had never seen her writing a letter. That was what Grandpa Thornton thanked Papa for!

He wished Mama had not been ashamed to admit she couldn't read. He would have helped her; they could have learned together, beginning with the first grade.

Why was he sympathizing? It was her lie, pretending she could read when she couldn't. He swiped his shirtsleeve across his eyes and nose. He'd show her. Bad as he felt, he would do every one of the dadgum problems.

Chapter 23

Go to bed, son," Papa said. Talmadge jerked himself awake, recalled that he had lain his head across his arms to rest a minute. It was dark now; Papa had lit the lamp.

"Yes, sir." He took his books into his room, put them on the chest of drawers, and was unbuckling his overalls when Dwight coughed. It so startled Talmadge that he jumped. "I didn't know you were in here," he said.

"I reckon I am," Dwight said. "Less this is somebody else laying here."

Talmadge sank into bed.

"I been thinking," Dwight said. "When the crop's in, I'm going to leave. But I won't run off in the night. I'll tell Papa straight out."

Before Missy's sickness, Talmadge thought, he wouldn't have understood. But now he knew what it must be like for Dwight. Dwight couldn't think, this is temporary. It will end and I'll go back to school.

Talmadge couldn't talk about it right now. The headache was really bad, his stomach was queasy, and he felt as if he had fever. He hadn't said the bedtime prayer in a long time. He ran it through his mind: Now I lay me down to sleep. I pray the Lord my soul to keep. If I should die before I wake.... "Dwight?"

"Yeah?"

"You know the agate Mr. Parks gave you? I took it to school. Stinky....I let it get cracked. I buried it on the ditch bank."

"I wondered what you did with it."

Talmadge sat up. "You knew I took it?"

"I knew when I heard about that blue agate you used as a shooter—even before I checked my drawer." Dwight yawned. "I considered giving you a pounding, but it was more fun watching you wrestle with your conscience."

Talmadge settled back down. Dwight had a mean streak, letting him worry and feel guilty when he knew all along. But that was okay. They were friends again. It had happened the night Dwight almost ran away.

"You ain't asked what I'm going to do when I leave."

"What're you going to do?"

"I'm going to join the Civilian Conservation Corps."

Talmadge knew about the CCC. It afforded a place to live, food, and clothes. The thirty dollars a month it paid was sent home to the parents. He knew of two boys from Limon who had joined up. "You're not old enough."

"I can pass for seventeen." After a minute, Dwight said, "It's not what I want to do. Planting trees and digging ditches is too much like farm work. But it's the only thing I can figure out. With the money that's sent home, Papa can hire a field hand to take my place."

Dwight's words seemed to be running together in his aching head. It was against the rules to take even aspirin without Mama or Papa's permission. He hated to ask; everybody would get alarmed if they knew he had fever and a headache. "What is it you want to do?"

"You laugh, you're dead. I want to be a draftsman. For machinery."

Talmadge tried to think of what he should say. But he didn't know what a draftsman was, much less how to go about being one.

Dwight laughed, if you could call the sound he made a laugh. "Fat chance." He turned over, his face to the wall.

The conversation was finished. Talmadge closed his eyes and took deep breaths.

Somebody was knocking at the front door. Papa was telling the person to come on in. Dr. Spain. Of course.

Who else would come to a house under quarantine?

"I won't disturb her," he heard Dr. Spain say. "In fact, Mr. and Mrs. McLinn, I'm here to talk to you."

They were coming into the kitchen.

"Don't make a fresh pot for me," Dr. Spain said. He sounded exhausted.

"It's already on," Papa said. "You want coffee, Roseanne?"

"No, thank you, Papa," Roseanne said.

"Mrs. Teasley sent us this here cake," Mama said. "It's mighty good."

"Just a small slice," Dr. Spain said.

Mama would give him a big slice.

The coffee was beginning to perk. The smell nauseated Talmadge. Oh, no! His stomach.... He was going to be sick. Talmadge jumped up, bolted through the door, through the kitchen, and across the back porch. He barely made it to the edge of the porch before he threw up.

Chapter 24

Dr. Spain sat in a chair beside Talmadge's bed. He had completed his examination, and a relieved smile touched his mouth. "Our boy has a mild case of grippe," he said. "The city doctors I've been talking with would call his case 'stomach flu.' "

Mama, Papa, Dwight, and Roseanne were all in the room: he saw the relief in their faces. They couldn't be any more relieved than he. Even while he had kept assuring himself that he didn't have infantile paralysis, he had been plenty worried. Now that he had vomited, he felt a lot better.

"It's common for at least one sibling in a family with an infantile paralysis case to get the grippe." Dr. Spain stood. "Suppose you all come into the kitchen."

Something was up, Talmadge thought, as he and Dwight put on their shirts and overalls.

When they were all seated at the table, Dr. Spain said, "Crippled Children's Hospital in Memphis will accept Missy. I'll take her as soon as the quarantine is over."

Except for Roseanne's drawn-in breath, there was no sound.

Finally, Papa said, "They won't turn her down we'uns can't pay right off? When the settling's done...." His voice trailed away.

"There will be no charge, Mr. McLinn," Dr. Spain said. "There are available funds for patients without means."

"We got relatives in Memphis," Mama said. "If they don't have a extra bed for me at that clinic, I can stay with them at night."

Dr. Spain shook his head. "I'm sorry, Mrs. McLinn, but you won't be able to stay with Missy. Visiting hours are limited."

Papa put his forefinger through his coffee cup handle, but he didn't lift the cup. "How long?"

"You can't put an exact time on the rehabilitation process," Dr. Spain said. "Several months. Possibly a year."

For a minute there was total silence, then Mama bent back her head and let out a low-pitched wail. Papa reached over and took her hand. "Easy, Pet. Hold on."

Talmadge already felt stunned, and the things that

were happening confused him. When they had first learned that Missy had infantile paralysis, Mama had been the strong one, and Papa had gone a little crazy. And now Mama had come apart, and Papa was the strong one.

Dr. Spain stood. "It will be hard on her at first. But she'll adjust. By the way, as soon as I lift the quarantine, the Teasleys and Clarks and others plan to give an hour after their workday to help you all catch up."

Papa left the table to see Dr. Spain out. The murmur of their voices floated from the front porch.

When he came back and sat down, Papa said, "Dr. Spain was telling me when he would come for Missy. And he said that once in a while him and his wife go into Memphis on Sunday afternoon. They'll give Mother and me a ride so we can visit Missy."

Talmadge closed his eyes. An hour or two on an occasional Sunday afternoon! Missy had never spent even one night away from her family. If they were there, in Memphis, she would at least be able to feel their nearness.

Dwight drew lines on the oilcloth with his thumbnail. He was not going to say that tractors would be taking over on Limon anyway.

Papa started to take a drink of his coffee, but his hand trembled and he set the cup back into the saucer.

"You're a fine carpenter, Papa," Roseanne said quietly. "Of course, there's not any guarantees, but there's not any with farming, either. We found that out in Wild Hog Holler."

Talmadge ran his fingers through his hair. He had been right about seeing fear on Papa's face the day he read the letter from Cousin Maybelle. The letter telling him there was building going on in Memphis. But he had been wrong about the reason Papa was scared. Papa wasn't afraid to move to Memphis. He wanted to go, and he wanted to do carpentry work, but he had grown up on a farm and had farmed ever since he and Mama married. He was afraid of failing if he tried a different field. Mama knew that, too.

Papa laid one hand on the table, lifted his cup with the other. His hands were steady now. He took a swallow of coffee, set the cup down, and said, "We can't go till after the settling, but considering the cotton opened early, I figure that'll come early, too. We'll sell off our stock and hire one of them hauling outfits in Willowboro to take our furnishings."

Scared or not, Papa was going. Talmadge put his own hands between his knees. His palms were sweating. Dwight had stopped drawing on the oilcloth. Dwight was looking at him, waiting. Dwight ought to be shouting with joy. He wouldn't have to join the CCC. He could get a job in Memphis. Maybe he could learn about drafting for machines. But Dwight was not shouting, or even smiling. He was waiting.

"Mama, Papa," Roseanne said, "I'm going to marry

Matt Williams after the crop is in."

Papa's face turned red; his eyes flashed, and he opened his mouth to speak.

"Don't say it, Papa," Roseanne said. "No, I haven't let him come around, and he hasn't been pleased about that. But seeing you level your gun on a man I liked discouraged me from letting Matt call on me proper."

"That man in Mississippi weren't no good!"

"He had a lot of goodness in him!"

"Hush," Mama said. "Both of you hush."

Talmadge ran his fingers through his hair. Roseanne was letting him know that he could live with her and Mr. Williams. That was why she had told Papa just now that she aimed to marry. Mama was saying something, talking to Papa about Roseanne.

"There comes a time for every bird to leave its nest," Mama said. "Just like I left mine for you, and you left yours for me. I don't want no enmity between us and our daughter and her family."

Papa looked down at his coffee cup, then lifted his head and said to Roseanne, "Mr. Williams has won hisself a good woman."

Tears welled in Roseanne's eyes. Mama nodded, then grief came back into her face. She was thinking about Missy again, worrying about her being in Memphis without them. Talmadge straightened his shoulders and said, "Papa. Mama. I'd like to go to Memphis when Missy does."

Chapter 25

When Dr. Spain lifted the quarantine, Talmadge went to school to return his books and say good-bye. Meg Weston got tears in her eyes, and Peadod cried outright. LaVerne said she had been to a movie theater in Memphis that was like a palace. "When you go to a picture show there, think of me and my poor pining heart," she said. "I envy you," John Edward said. "There are bound to be fine libraries in a big city like Memphis."

A lot of the people in his class said they would write to him, but he knew it was over. Without regular care, friendships soon withered.

That night after supper, he paced the kitchen while

Mama wiped the oilcloth. Dr. Spain would be coming for Missy and him tomorrow morning at five o'clock. "Maybe I ought to check the suitcase again," he said.

"If you and Roseanne left out anything, we'uns will bring it when we come for a Sunday visit." Now she was wiping the cookstove. "Don't worry about Jasper. Roseanne's going to take over the care of him." She dipped the cloth in the dishwater, wrung it out. "Mind Maybelle and Mr. Parks."

"Yes, ma'am. I will."

"It was mighty nice of Mr. Parks to say you could work at his store after school and on Saturday."

Talmadge nodded.

"'Course, if you was to work full-time...." Leaving the sentence unfinished, she caught his eyes with hers.

"I aim to keep going to school, Mama," he said quietly but firmly.

Her lips tightened, and she picked up the broom and started sweeping the kitchen. She probably knew that his volunteering to go to Memphis when Missy did was not totally unselfish. Yes, it would reassure Missy to know he was there. And he could contribute more by working part-time for cash than he could by picking cotton part-time. He could study the newspaper advertisements for workers and send them to Papa and Dwight, start looking for a house. The selfish part was that it would be easier on him to start at a new school early in the school year.

"You're glad to be moving to Memphis, aren't you, Mama?" he said. "I mean, even if Missy hadn't of gotten sick, you'd be glad to move there, wouldn't you?"

"I'd move there without a argument for no other reason than it's what your daddy wants to do. But yes, it'll be nice to visit with Maybelle. And there's Methodist churches there."

"Those the only two reasons you can think of?"

"No," she said. "There's another one. While it won't be like home, we'll at least be back in Tennessee."

He had hoped she might say something about opportunity, which would maybe open the door to her understanding about school. But Mama hadn't changed; he doubted that she ever would. "You want me to sweep the back porch?" he asked.

"That would be mighty nice," she said, and handed him the broom.

He went through the screen door onto the porch. Wearing the new shoes today had been like breaking them in all over again; the sun warmth lingering in the porch boards felt good to his bare feet.

When he had finished sweeping, he set the broom against the wall and stood looking out at the lot and the barn and the land. The days were getting shorter; dusk was stealing across the fields. The fragrance of dying supper fires floated on the air, and whippoorwills greeted each other with their loud, clear calls.

Talmadge took out his harmonica and softly played

random notes. He was scared; he was confident. He was sad; he was excited. Explorers, he thought, must have experienced such a mixture of feelings on the eve of a great adventure.